The Home Jar

STORIES

The Home Jar

STORIES

Nancy Zafris

SWITCHGRASS BOOKS   NORTHERN ILLINOIS UNIVERSITY PRESS   DeKalb

This is a work of fiction. All characters are products of the author's imagination, and any resemblance to persons living or dead is entirely coincidental.

Library of Congress Cataloging-in-Publication Data

Zafris, Nancy.

The home jar : stories / Nancy Zafris.

pages cm

Summary: "Zafris is a critically acclaimed writer because of the highly distinctive, piercing intelligence that underlies her works. This book gathers some of her short stories that are laugh-out-loud funny one moment and bittersweet the next"—

Provided by publisher.

ISBN 978-0-87580-688-4 (pbk.) — ISBN 978-1-60909-081-4 (e-book)

1. Humorous stories. I. Title.

PS3576.A285H66 2013

813'.54—dc23   2012045137

This work is dedicated to

Lewis Nordan

Rich Unger

Tula Gounaris

Contents

Acknowledgments

Over the past several years I have been creatively inspired and blessed by the participants, staff, and friends who make up The Kenyon Review Summer Adult Workshops, and I thank everyone wholeheartedly. In particular, I wish to acknowledge Trish Walsh, for generously providing details for the story "A Modlified Cylinder," and Lori White for spurring on "White's Lake." I am grateful to the National Endowment for the Arts and the Ohio Arts Council for their support during the writing of these stories. Finally, much gratitude to my editor, Mark Heineke, for his enthusiastic support of literary writing and the short story.

**The stories in this book were published previously
by the following magazines:**

"Stealing the Llama Farm," *The Kenyon Review*;

"Prix Fixe," *Glimmer Train*;

"Swimming in the Dark," *The Missouri Review*;

"Furgus Welcomes You," *The Journal*;

"The Home Jar," *Prairie Schooner*;

"A Modified Cylinder," *River Styx*;

"After Lunch," *Prairie Schooner*;

Acknowledgments

"If A Then B Then C," orig. pub. as "Nothing"
in *The Kenyon Review Online*;

"Vantage Point," *Arts & Letters*;

"Digging the Hole," *New England Review*;

"White's Lake," *Five Points*

The Home Jar

STORIES

Stealing the Llama Farm

THERE CAME A DAY WHEN I stole the llama farm from
Amy Boyd. I was in love with Amy Boyd and once long ago I had
saved her father's life and felt the sun charge through my body. I
think almost everyone would say I was not the kind of person who
would steal someone's llama farm right out from under them, but
whatever made me do it must have been waiting there inside me.

Amy Boyd was the first smart woman I'd ever met, at least to my
knowledge, which didn't kick in until twenty years had passed. When
it finally did it was like all the desire from the lower half of my body
moved upwards to my head. I wanted to express to her what this felt
like but the words could not be found in the tangle of my brain, the
jungle in there having been tended all these years by the many dumb
women, starting with my mother, who had set about watering it. Not
that I lay my troubles on these women, but they didn't help.

Besides running the llama farm Amy Boyd wrote stories, and
all her stories had llamas in them: llamas giving birth to other
llamas, llamas passing on the wisdom of llamas, llamas wondering
what to do with themselves, biorhythmic llamas, llamas practicing
euthanasia on other llamas. I said "Amy, put some people in these
stories" and Amy Boyd didn't like hearing that. But, for example,
you don't see movies with venetian blinds as the main characters,
two venetian blinds trying to adopt a tiny solid-white blind for
their little baby window in the bathroom. You don't see that in the
movies — maybe there's a reason.

As usual Amy didn't answer me. I was starting to see what my two ex-wives had found so annoying about me. "You should be glad I don't argue," I'd told them. "I'm just a mellow guy." But now there was nothing more I would have liked than a heated discussion leading to a heated argument. "Well, let's just talk about it," I suggested to Amy. "Maybe you have seen a movie about venetian blinds. Have you? Amy?"

But she had pulled on her rubber knee-highs and was already out the door. I followed her to the llama barns and we passed the hallowed circle where I had saved her father's life, her father now long dead so what had been the point of saving him, really, a waste of a perfectly good foot that had not yet seen its prime. Amy was careful to avoid this permanent dead image in the grass where it had happened. It softened her some, I could see by the slump of her shoulders, to remember her father and how he would have died a little bit earlier if not for me, just a little bit earlier, that little bit of extra time hardly worth mentioning now, but how were we to divine such a thing on that day, how were we to know he might not have a life dull and interminable ahead of him. God knows he had been dull and interminable up to that point. There was no reason to think it might not continue.

The dead spot in the grass, still recognizably shaped to the imaginative eye as a lower torso, set my foot to clawing inside its boot, and when my foot hurt like that it felt like something punching its way out of a box and only a sturdy box could contain it, which is why I always cage my feet in cowboy or steel-toed work boots. I couldn't help but look up as we passed the spot where it happened; I can't help looking up everywhere I go, and everywhere I notice the same thing: how low the high tension wires are, how low they hover, how low certain death is strung out above us.

Amy's father had been struggling with his new extension ladder, showing off how to carry something forty-feet long, and was heading straight toward these wires. And when I ran to push him away both his clenched hands knocked back from the ladder flicking one of mine against it, and what was in that wire shot through my arm and fired out my foot. The whole town drove by to check out the scorch burns on the grass and for more than a month I got a happy buzz out of my charred foot and was proud of the two toes I was going to lose, and my twenty-one year old self had plenty of time to perfect the many jokes about what to do with those toes. Then the skin grafts and rehab started. By then the miracle of simply being alive had receded into the forgotten background where daily living day after day always managed to put it and I was in a terrible misery compounded by morphine addiction and I vowed then and it's a vow I've kept that I had done my good deed for the afternoon and anybody else bearing a ladder toward a high tension wire was on their own. I'd yell out, sure, try to get their attention, but that's as far as it would go — unless of course it was Amy Boyd and then I would sacrifice all.

I trailed Amy to the llama barns where she began scooping food pellets from a bin. A false spring had passed and we were back to winter again. Amy said another big snowstorm was sweeping over the Great Lakes. I thought less about the snowstorm and more about the fact that Amy had freely offered a line of conversation. "Pedro!" she then hollered, sounding mean. The llamas began shuffling toward the food, her beloved Pedro, Jésus, and Maria, the three llamas she talked about most; then Felipe, Carmita, and Sean. A half dozen more after that. Their number had dwindled since her father's day when almost a hundred roamed the place — it was hard, however, to call that time a heyday. So many ugly llamas and something extra and human, a low-hanging unhappiness, had brought a scrounging kind of gloom to the place. The Boyd farm was without topsoil or beauty and eventually it had caused Amy's mother to go AWOL with Amy's little brothers, and Amy was left alone with her father until she went off to college at Miami University. I thought Oxford, Ohio would claim her for good, but two years after graduation her dad was dead and the English major was back to save the farm.

I backed away from the barn. I positioned myself at a safe distance from the llamas shoving in to eat. Don't even get me started on llamas and how much I hate them. Llamas bite, they hiss and spit, they lay down and get a mood on and won't get up, they're ugly, they kick, from a distance they look like ostriches, up close they look like llamas, they have no social graces, they bite, they have not a jot of affability, they bite, they refuse to look you in the eye, they bite, if you attempt friendly eye contact they spit at you, if you do worse and flash a smile at them they turn around and release their dung at your feet. I've seen this happen too many times not to know it for a fact.

And it wasn't as if the llamas liked Amy but hated the rest of us. They appeared to hate her, too. They saved some of their best spitting and kicking and biting just for her, just for their Amy. It was a sick hostile dependence between Amy and her llamas, and despite a compelling case of domestic abuse up and down her arms, bite marks on her thighs and quail egg hematomas on her calves, she stuck it out, she spent her days caring for them and her nights writing about them, hunched over in the dark with pencils that kept breaking she pressed so hard, writing stories about my arch rivals Pedro, Felipe, and Jésus — why did smart women get sucked into these kinds of relationships? With me it was easy, I married dumb, we were two shallow wells and when our wells ran dry, there were no permanent hard feelings, just a need to fill up elsewhere — it didn't seem so bad so I tried it all over again, and life moved on.

It was past five o'clock and I had to be going. For the 500th time I asked Amy if she wanted to meet up at Chi-Chi's — *meet up* was how I always said it, not a date, just two cars happening upon each other in the same lot, a meeting up. For the 500th time Amy didn't bother to answer me and I headed for my truck, rehearsing a final positive remark about Pedro (*good appetite tonight!*) so I would be welcomed back into her good graces the next day without having to limp for it, when I turned and saw Amy's eyes glaring right at me, sunken and black. It had been so long since I had seen them focused my way, I welcomed their fierce glare, my heart rose at the sight. I loved everything about her, even her eye sockets tunneling to a hateful squint, because everything about her was nothing I'd ever known. I can't say it was good, I can't say it was bad. It was something I ignored for twenty years.

"Yes or no?" she was demanding. "Are you going to do it or not?"

"Well yeah," I said. "Absolutely. What time do you wanna meet up?"

At Chi-Chi's that night I sat alone. Ours was a town of 8700 though it felt like fifty, all of that fifty usually hanging out at Chi-Chi's every night. To my knowledge Amy had never been inside and she had just increased her streak by another cipher. She had not wanted to eat with me. She had wanted me to take care of her llamas while she drove to Pittsburgh to pick up her brother at the airport; she was sure she'd get caught in a snowstorm and have to stay the night. She asked me to feed Pedro and the others but she never said please to me, she never said thank you. She was losing all her manners. She hardly ever made eye contact. I had to dance in a ring to keep up with her averted stares.

Chi-Chi's was the only restaurant to speak of in the town. It was three years old and had quickly driven out of business the only other major restaurant — a smorgasbord with a coal mining motif that surprisingly was not named The Black Lung Buffet. We had turned away from all-you-can-eat and strip mining; we had embraced Mexico and Mexico had embraced us.

"Ready to order?" the waitress asked. Still in high school, she wore somebody's varsity jacket over her uniform — somebody from Steubenville. "Do you want to hear the specials?"

"No, just give me the Hearty Ole!," I said.

It embarrassed me even to say it. I dreamed of a time when no one bothered to order off the Chi-Chi menu anymore and the sweet broad faces of the waitresses had to press back a smile at the mention of chimichangas. We ate simple and pure, *arroz y pollo* or, if we got lucky, *arroz y llama,* and one of us, afterwards, always drove to the house where the person he loved lived alone with her creatures and he stretched out on her grass picking the charmed scorched spot for his bed. And for the rest of the night whatever he dreamed belonged to him.

The next morning I drove to Amy's farm. She was already gone. Her note told me Pedro and pals had been fed. The crabbed handwriting seemed to scowl as fiercely as she did, no mention of a thank you, no mention of a please, no mention of a help yourself to tap water for doing this, but at the end of this sour note she had drawn a big smiley face with a single spitcurl on top and one above each ear. That big smiley face with three hairs hit me hard with anger. It propelled me to the pantry where I sorted through the keys hanging on the key jockey and found the one to the ancient stake-body truck. I had to excavate the equipment barn to clear a path for it; then I drove it to the llama field and loaded as many of those animals as I could on it. They kept trying to bite me. Their matted fleeces gave me a coughing fit. I took off my belt and flailed and coughed and yanked them to the truck. I had to hope that special llama mood wouldn't strike because if they decided to belly down on me I'd never be able to budge them off the ground. But I got six of them loaded up in that ancient truck without any hissing or spitting. Their necks rested over the boards I had, one long-ago summer, staked into the flat bed for Amy's father, and for the moment at least they seemed content enough.

I looked across the Boyd farm. A line of dark junipers rose from the damaged land. Strip-mining had drawn our horizon ragged and had forever shifted the landscape; now neither its beauty nor its ugliness was natural. I felt I was living a lie in a landscape that itself was carved into a lie. And you might well say to this, you might say, Why didn't you simply extricate yourself from the lie, why didn't you leave? But that's just it, that's the thing. Why didn't I leave, why don't I now? That's the point, isn't it?

I got in the truck and drove off. I knew of a gravel pit in front of Wilma Lipinski's deserted place and I turned into the the dirt road heading there. The house stood on a moraine. Gravel pit operations had been threatening to swallow it for years, but the house still stood. I drove down into Wilma's gravel pit with a ton and a quarter's worth of llamas and there I had to unload them one by one. Then I went back for another truckful and it was afternoon before I was done. The sun was clouded over. Snow flurries flickered the grayness; the light was already preparing to leave. The door to the empty Lipinski house was gone, I saw. The windows were broken into glass daggers. I could see some stuff still inside. I wondered if Amy knew about the love affair her father was having with Wilma before his not-so-old heart, for once fighting out of its bag of dullness, stopped just like that. The wind was blowing in a stronger snow. Amy had been right about the weather. I walked back to the truck and retrieved her rifle and a box of 30–06 cartridges.

I would have started with Pedro if he hadn't been bunched in the pack. I took aim at his protective circle. One shot, one llama down, one echo rolling back, and with each crack of the rifle my love for Amy Boyd grew. The Ruger 77 was burning up my hands with only five llamas dropped, but I'd known a burning much worse, much worse, and I kept going. Maria's front hooves had made it over the lip of the pit when I got her — that doomed, frantically stubborn gal was more like Amy than any of them. The rest just stood there like the dumb llamas they were. Jésus waited calmly, true to his namesake, and hiding behind him but not for long was Pedro — for once his raggedy hide shone. Inside my shaking boot a three-toed foot that hardly belonged to me was spewing a geyser of pain and fire and clawing to get out. The gray sun was reduced to a scrap of driftwood but once the whole of that bright star had traveled through me.

One shot, one llama down, one echo rolling back. I had never killed so many things in a row and been able to take my time about it, my own good time that was my own secret song I was now discovering, and if I had a soul it was awakening. The rhythm was powerful as the morphine and just as quick in its addiction, and when I was finished with the llamas I turned my sights on Wilma Lipinski's house and saw people from the town inside, people I liked, and I shot every one of them with the rest of Amy's cartridges.

Then I went to Chi-Chi's. I knew the limp had started. I sat at a table hoping to be alone but already some of the guys I had killed were patting me on the back and saying hey how's it going. One of them said, with only mild interest, "Didn't I see you shooting some llamas over at the Lipinski place?" I said, "Coulda been." I held onto my cup of coffee. I looked down at my burning hands. I said to myself, Now what are you going to do? Are you going to do something with your life or are you going to sit here and drink coffee for the rest of its unfolding?

Right on cue the high school waitress, in somebody's Steubenville varsity jacket, came to my table holding up her glass pot. The young chubbiness of her face hid all the bones, and she could have been Mexican, or Mayan, or even Asian. She asked, "Warm it up?" and I said yes, honey, just keep it coming for the rest of my life, coffee coffee coffee, coffee till my brain explodes and drips back south where it belongs.

If I couldn't have her, no one would, that's what the world would be saying in two days when Amy started packing and called in her brothers to help her move. The snowstorm would be bringing with it a wretched gift of pain for my foot and when everybody was at the height of talking about me I would be limping my worst and trying not to show it, which would show it even more. Once I had saved a man, it was a hundred years ago, and now I would save his daughter. There was no reason for this, it was just something I wanted to do. If I couldn't have her, then someone would. I'd sent her on her way.

Swimming in the Dark

LIFE IS STRANGE, ISN'T IT? A hotel pool in Rome, the china plate of blue water, fifteen other girls in the company-issue swimsuit. We're stewardesses from Japan. Yesterday we went shopping. Tomorrow, Singapore.

Our lounge chairs surround the pool like a fence, a red fence splashed with white. Next to me Michie talks of wanting to wear a bikini. She is the one who wears the most make-up in our group and that is saying something. When we're primped for a flight we look more like a troupe of Kabuki actors. Too much makeup and somehow you begin to look like a man. It's the layers of foundation on our faces, but that's how they like us, painted in white, the post-adolescent pimples hidden. The cosmetics clog the pores, causing further pimples, then more layers to cover up, and *voila!* in no time I'm admiring a pretty transvestite in the mirror.

Make-up free, I turn my face up to the sun. I have my eyes closed and I'm getting hot. Beside me Michie sighs. "*Omiyage,*" she laments.

"Such a constant trial," agree the others.

Already I have three shopping bags of calfskins and Gucci from Via Condotti, presents for family, in-laws, and friends, but hidden in one of the bags is a secret treat for myself: miniature yellow post-its with an inch of Paloma Picasso leather binding, on sale for fifty euros. There are so many presents to buy for others, and so many international trips we take, each trip requiring another round of *omiyage*. But the Paloma Picasso post-its are for me; they made the laborious day of shopping worthwhile.

Even now, relaxing beside the pool, money spent and obligations fulfilled, we are still waiting to enjoy ourselves. The blue pool is untouched, a sheet of glass, brittle when we look at it, deadly if we dare to shatter its surface. The only ripples come from the murmurs that begin to rise like heat shimmies from the sunbathing bodies.

"Let's dive in," suggests someone.

I don't immediately recognize her voice so I open my eyes. Of course. It's Hisako. Typical. She's the mischievous one, a hostess in the third cabin.

A couple of others concur. "It's so hot," they say. "She won't mind."

"Do you think she is sleeping?" asks another.

"I could call her on the phone," suggests Michie. "Ask if she is coming down?"

"Not you, Michie." We laugh, then turn quickly around, spooked and fearful, half-expecting an apparition of Ishihara-san to waver before us. Everyone knows our supervisor cares least for Michie though she is diligent and obedient. Michie comes from the north, a small village in Hokkaido. Her skin is like an icy blue pearl; she seems different, a product of the cold. I don't know why Ishihara-san dislikes her; perhaps it is her country upbringing, perhaps it is her large mouth neoned in a prostitute's oxblood lipstick.

One would think Ishihara-san would disapprove of the mischievous Hisako, but Hisako, it is well-known, comes from a wealthy Tokyo family. She is a member of an exclusive tennis club, and Ishihara-san is salivating for an invitation. In another ten months Hisako will quit. She is to be married next May. Having been courted by so many suitors has made her a little arrogant, fearless of consequences. Now that the airline has loosened its rules, almost a quarter of the stewardesses are married like me. But it is still hoped that we abide by the former rule and retreat into housewifedom.

Boredom. I am bored. It's hardly a violent experience. Then it would at least have something to recommend it. It's more like being waterlogged and drowning from the inside out. Inside me lives a stranger but I've never met her. All I know is that she isn't married.

The sun heats our disagreement about whether to jump into the pool ahead of our supervisor. Our disagreement wanders aimlessly, like a victim of heat stroke. "Ishihara-san is so old," says one of the girls. "I know she's already thirty."

"No, she's twenty-eight," asserts another girl in a peevish tone.

"Let's not argue." This from Fumiko, the leader of our pep talks. "Our lack of togetherness will show on tomorrow's flight." Fumiko's zealous dutifulness shows on her face, overshadowing any attractiveness. Her features are suffused with good intentions. How annoying she is!

"I still have *omiyage* to buy," whines Michie in misery.

"We all have *omiyage* to buy," says Fumiko. "It's a blessed obligation to show our appreciation to family and friends."

"I don't need to appreciate them every two weeks," says Michie with a frigid blast of Hokkaido wisdom.

"She's right," one of the other girls says. "This present-giving is a painful chore."

"No one likes it but we have to do it."

"They just tuck the presents away into some cranny with hardly a glance. And our apartments are so small! I have nowhere to put the presents I receive."

"Admit it," says Michie. "You rewrap them and give them away." Embarrassed silence.

"We are complaining too much," Fumiko admonishes. "And you, Michie, you like buying presents for yourself, why not others?"

That heats up the argument even more. It is silly to discuss such a thing since the custom of present-giving will not change. But this is the sort of useless squabble we carry on all the time. The argument is orderly, each person taking a turn while the others listen attentively, allowing an appropriate gap of silence before another one begins to speak so that no one appears to be jumping in out of turn... the very tradition of this squabbling is comforting — or at least it puts me to sleep. I lie back, their words fueling the rhythms of oncoming dreams as I begin to drift off.

Amidst the steady ebb and flow of Japanese comes the rushed slur of English. This intrigues me. I am anxious to see what my dream holds.

All of a sudden several of the girls squeak in horror and my pleasant dream is interrupted never to be recaptured. I open my eyes. Above me a weather balloon is floating fast, floating downward, plummeting toward the glassy surface of the pool. How long have I slept? Minutes or blocks of minutes? Or just seconds? Funny, this is what confuses me. Not the question, Why is a weather balloon floating into a hotel pool? That seems perfectly natural.

The horrified squeaking of some of the girls turns to chortling as the brass ballast of the weather balloon pierces the surface of the pool and sinks to the bottom. Flood warning! flood warning! signals the little balloon. Italian weather reports — humph — now I know why not to trust them.

But I wasn't dreaming the English I heard. I hear it again, clearly spoken. A group is rushing up the hill through the bushes, destroying, by the sound of it, everything in their paths. They arrive breathless, leaves and twigs pasted onto their wet faces, the sweat pouring like tears down their cheeks. "Oh my god," a woman in the group cries, covering her mouth at the sight of the sunken balloon.

"Don't worry, don't worry," a man calms her, blocking her passage with an outstretched arm. "I'll get it."

The girls turn to me to translate. "Well, there's nothing much to translate so far," I tell them.

"They've lost their balloon," Michie explains to the group.

"Buy another," Hisako says sarcastically, emboldened somehow by the Americans' presence. Everyone shushes her. *Spoiled rich girl,* the Americans might say if they could understand her. But they're probably rich themselves. Why else would they be in Rome.

In my hotel room inside a shopping bag are Paloma Picasso post-its for fifty euros. What kind of message is worthy for these yellow squares? *Watanabe-san called. Please call him back.* Is that a message worthwhile enough? If I calligraph it with brush and ink, my miniature red seal in the corner, is that a good enough message for Paloma Picasso?

There are five in the group of Americans. The woman who has spoken is blonde, now quite a dirty blonde; perspiration has darkened her roots and flattened out any hair-sprayed body. The man comforting her is handsome and I am moved by his good looks as well as something else, a gentleness. There is one other woman and two other men.

"Hello, ladies," the handsome man addresses us.

The women of his group are wearing dark dresses and high heels. The men wear white shirts and ties and ironed khaki pants.

"Hello. How are you?" we reply in unison.

Yellow paper squares for fifty euros. They were on sale. Use them up, I tell myself. They're cheap, fifty euros, half the usual price. Use them up without a care.

"Would one of you, since you're already suited up that is, mind diving into the pool and retrieving that canister?"

"What?" the girls ask me blankly.

I will never use post-its that cost fifty euros, I realize. I will never let anyone else use them.

What's he saying now?" the girls demand.

"Nothing," I tell them.

The man regards our mute stares. How strange we must look to him in our matching bathing suits arrayed on a chain of matching lounge chairs. I think of the coffin hotels for commuters — in Tokyo everything, everywhere, is somehow an arrangement of identical cubicles. Does he find us laughable? A handsome, gentle man like him — what could he be thinking of us?

"We are waiting for our supervisor before we go in the pool," I finally explain. "If you would like to wait..."

"Oh my god," the blonde woman says, holding back a sob. Mascara runs down, and her black eyes match the collapse of her hair.

"What is it?" I ask him. "A weather balloon?"

"Uhh, a weather balloon... No, not exactly."

Michie is tugging on my arm. "What, what!"

"Nothing," I tell her.

The handsome man begins to loosen his tie and slip it over his head, loop intact. He hands it to the second woman. Next he takes off his shirt. "Sorry, ladies," he says as he begins unzipping his pants, but as for me I'm thinking, *Keep on going*.

He wears blue Calvin Klein briefs. His socks are the last to come off, and then he dives in.

"American men are hairy," Hisako says with disgust.

"At least they're able to have beards," one of the girls offers.

"Who would want a man who could grow a beard?" another protests. "They scratch."

"You would shave it every day."

"Some don't."

This is threatening to develop into another of our pointless squabbles, but then the man surfaces with a belching gasp and we fall silent.

"It's because they eat so much meat," one of the girls ventures, but the argument has fizzled. All eyes are on the man. He pulls himself out of the pool, hands the brass canister trailing a shriveled balloon to the blonde woman, who is sobbing noiselessly with her mouth pushed shut, and then he turns to us. His eyes are wet and blue, and his lashes sparkle.

Keep your clothes off for awhile, I think.

"Could I dry off with one of your towels?" he asks. "I'm very sorry to bother you."

We gape at him wide-eyed, without response.

"Someone so hairy, on my towel..." Hisako sucks in her breath, as though in pain. Ever since her engagement, she has become more vocal against Americans, leaving me to wonder if she didn't have a secret wish to marry a rich, good-looking Californian with a nice nose and big eyes, someone, in fact, who looks exactly like the man addressing us.

"Just stand there, you'll dry," the second woman in his group tells him.

"Well, what do we do now?" one of the men asks. "Let's just scatter him over the Piazza Navona. He always liked that place."

"He did not," the second woman says indignantly.

The blonde woman's head dips over the brass canister, her shoulders droop, and it looks as though she might drop to the ground and fold into herself. She is still crying convulsively, making no sound. The veins are bulging down her forehead.

"It didn't work," says the handsome man, dripping wet in his briefs. His voice is low and sympathetic and he touches her elbow. "We'll have to scatter him."

"No!" the blonde woman cries.

"You could save him," the second woman suggests. "On a nice shelf or something."

"What is going on?" Michie asks.

"Quiet," I tell her.

"Tell me, what is going on? Why is the woman crying?"

"It's nothing," I tell her.

"She's crying because the balloon is popped," Michie explains to the others.

Now I've missed part of the conversation. The man is tugging his khakis over his wet body, saying, "All right, Freda, we'll get some more balloons."

"The woman's name is Freda," I tell Michie, hoping that will satisfy her.

"The woman's name is Freda," she tells the others.

"But how will we know where it lands?" the second woman asks.

"It's not supposed to land," Freda says.

"Which woman is Freda?" the girls ask me.

"The blonde one."

"Not very pretty, is she?" Hisako says.

"Hush!" the girls say.

"Well, you know it's going to land somewhere," the handsome man is telling Freda.

"It will never land!" Freda cries emphatically.

"Freda thinks the new balloon will never land," I tell them.

"She's nuts," Hisako says. "Not pretty."

With that the group marches off, a glum, grief-stricken brigade, not down the hill where they came from but through the hotel garden, leaving me to translate this sorry absurd event into something my co-workers can handle.

Sunbathing by a pool in the midday heat, my mind dulled by dreams, I have just watched a man's burial urn sail from the sky and land at my feet. What should I tell the others? That they've witnessed a poolside exhumation?

I decide to ask them what they think has happened. "It was a type of toy helicopter," one of the girls suggests. "Yes, that was it," they all immediately agree.

Consensus creates a new reality, a reality sealing a tiny whirly-bird motor in a brass container rather than the ashes of a dead man. Is it any less real? If it satisfies their curiosity, then isn't it just as good?

It is good enough for me. I simply want to go swimming.

I know no one will enter a pool contaminated by a burial urn. I'm queasy enough doing it myself. But I'll do it. I'm becoming desperately hot, and now I see Ishihara-san marching toward us, officious even in a long hotel robe that covers her red bathing suit slashed with white. She is quite a bit taller than average and wears her hair short, parted on the side. It's a business style, without adornment. On our flights she wears less make-up than the rest of us. She is not there to please the passengers; she is in charge of us, towering a head above, her business hairstyle ordering us about without words. Already I can feel myself breathing the artificial air. Tomorrow I will be packed into a 747 cylinder, my whole being pounded with the sonic white noise of silence. We'll feed the passengers, then pull the window shades and let them sleep. The fresh air I breathe every five minutes will be mixed with recirculated air; only my corpuscles will ever know the difference and they're not telling.

Ishihara-san unties her robe, apologizing for the delay. She is all smiles, with an extra beam directed to wealthy, tennis-playing Hisako, until she notices the pool. Someone has jumped in before her: small circles still spread lazily across the surface despite the man's exit several minutes earlier, and on the far side a suspicious trail of wet spots on the cement catches her attention. Ishihara-san immediately scans our bodies, giving Michie an extra hard look, an icy glare right out of Hokkaido. But here we are, everyone dry as burdock. So she jumps in, and with glee the rest of us follow. No water has ever felt better.

Oh, the post-its, I think. Fifty euros for post-its. Only once could I ever make myself defile them for a message: *Paloma Picasso called. Please call her back.*

I return to the pool after dark. I lie back on the lounge chair and look up at the sky. The city lights ignite the horizon, not in a

fiery way like Tokyo, but softly. Still, it's enough to do the damage.
I can't see the stars.

I think of this haiku:

> Everyone is asleep
> There is nothing to come between
> The moon and me

It isn't true. There is plenty of interference.

In the pool two lovers kiss. They splash daintily, like birds in a
birdbath. One could sit for several minutes without realizing they
are there.

A man lies on his back along the diving board. He appears to
be asleep. A couple sit on a bench in the garden, gazing into each
other's faces. In the darkness they look like statues.

Here comes the drunken march of the English language.
Interrupting this peaceful scene is the American group again. They
are making plans. Their beer bottles clang noisily against each
other. "I owe it to him, man," says a male voice.

"Let's fucking send him off."

As though vexed by the bad language, the man on the diving
board rolls over in troubled sleep. He plops into the pool.

"That woke him up," one of the American women say.

"Let's do it." The voice belongs to the handsome man. "What
do you say, Freda?"

"Fuck, yeah," says a giddy Freda.

Another big splash, right on cue.

"Watch it, you'll drown the poor guy."

Loud American laughter follows. Their grief has vanished, their
glumness replaced with an exhilarating love.

I was in love with someone once. He was not a college graduate and he wasn't the man I married. The man I married I met in

an *omiae*. The meeting was arranged by my father's brother who worked in a large bank as supervisor to my husband-to-be. All I heard about him was that he had gone to Kyoto University — straight — in a single try of the entrance exam. He was quite a catch. My mother was shrill with excitement, my father nearly dictatorial after the fiasco with my brother, whom they now seldom spoke of. My brother had barely started his first year of post-high school preparatory school, having failed all his entrance exams, when he dropped out and took a part-time job. My parents would never say what the job was.

The boy I was really in love with was an actor. His roles were on the stage, not television, and to get to the theaters you had to wind through narrow streets far from the major subway stops, calling into a public bath or soba shop to ask directions. One evening I saw him perform dressed only in a G-string and painted white. Everyone on stage was naked except for the G-string, and the white paint covered even the women's dark nipples. In the middle of the performance the actors stepped down from the stage and sidled up the aisle, using the arrested stealth of Nōh dance but adding a modern touch: they picked on the audience. They selected a victim innocently sitting in a seat for which he had paid and received a ticket, and they locked him in their gaze and stared at him until the victim began to squirm and shift, followed by those around him, the discomfort passed on down the line of audience members until finally a long, brightly-clothed row was rippling like a Chinese dragon. Then they crept on to someone else. My heart pounded as the white bodies stole up the aisle, and like everyone I wanted to flee. The boy I loved approached my row. He was so close I could see the cracks in his white paint. He pointed, and his eyes fastened onto me, but they were blank, staring through me, and it was then I realized he was only acting.

Not long afterwards I was walking with my future husband, still trying to talk myself out of love with the boy who painted himself white, and we strolled along Kabukicho, past the illicit theaters, turkish baths, and pachinko parlors. In front of the shows stood young men dressed in cheap tuxedos who called to the passersby about the merits of each of their stage presentations. They were in competition with each other, and they yelled as loudly as the vegetable and fish vendors in marketplaces, and sometimes came out and grabbed the men, trying to win their interest by pulling them inside. Calling in front of one of the porno theaters stood someone I knew despite the outfit and the hair teased back in a pompadour: my brother. He was approaching my future husband to lure him inside, but in an instant he turned and clapped the shoulder of someone else. His glance had been brief and empty. We walked past. I didn't look back, and we never acknowledged each other. When I saw him for New Year's, I introduced my future husband as a Kyoto University *straight* graduate and he asked my brother what he did. My brother said, "Part-time job" and that was as far as the questions went. Had anybody asked me, which they did not, I would have said I had no idea what he did for a living. And why should it matter? Does the American in the brass canister care about my brother's employment? And do we care about the American's? Is there a gold label on the canister inscribed, *He had a good job? He was a banker who graduated from Kyoto University and never made anybody happy.*

There they go again, the Americans winding through the garden and back into the hotel. I hitch onto their swaying Chinese dragon and follow them across the lobby and out the front door. I congratulate myself on my impulsiveness. Fumiko and the others are tucked inside their rooms. Ha! If they only knew what I was up to.

The men in the group are dressed in Bermuda shorts and polo shirts. They have on sneakers without socks. The two women wear sleeveless blouses tucked into linen shorts; they have on white sandals. Freda carries a large handbag that looks like two prayer rugs sewn together.

They stride full-tilt into the first bar they come to. It takes me several minutes to get up my nerve to follow. As I'm about to enter, out they come. Then it's full tilt into a second bar. This time I'm right behind them. I go to the other end of the counter and order a limonata to cool myself off. It's cooler than it was this afternoon, of course, but it is still a very hot night. The handsome man's shirt (his back is to me so I can stare) reveals a splash of droplets between the shoulder blades. A tide of perspiration rises from Freda's beltline, and the other woman's as well. I can hear Hisako complaining about this aspect of Americans, too. In our job we are not allowed to sweat. We're a Kabuki troupe of actors with exaggerated femininity who can perform a flight safety demonstration like a dance. Without sweating. Try to get an American stewardess to do that.

Our routine is this: My partner and I stand side by side in front of the passengers. All our gestures are perfectly synchronized, the oxygen masks pulled out like twin trombones. We even look alike, down to the lipstick in the exact same shade, identically applied with lip liner. (Poor Chieko, Michie's partner, oxblooded to match her Hokkaido roommate. The two whores in cabin four, we call them).

In the third bar, before I can order, a glass of red wine is set down before me. I was thinking more of an espresso, something to keep me awake. When I try to pay, the bartender grunts and gestures toward the group of Americans, none of whom are glancing my way. I take only a sip or two before the Americans move on, but in the fourth bar I drink it down, and it hits me.

They don't waste any time. Already they're out the door. A sleepy misdirection thickens their walk. Each one staggers ahead, sometimes draped over another's shoulder in a best friend embrace, but the humanity is accidental. I sense them growing further and further apart, becoming the very thing each one is seeking to avoid: alone.

They are way ahead of me in terms of drinks, but after the fifth bar I feel the same clumsy lethargy seeping through my limbs. I'm afraid I'll lose them. And I have no idea where I am. In the sixth bar I rush in ahead and order my espresso. Better. More alert. But I still don't know where I am.

In the seventh bar I long to sit down. I don't dare take the chance and besides, all seats are taken. The bar is jumping with excitement. Jump jump jump. Here I am, standing still.

She wrote with abandon on Paloma Picasso post-its and was able to demonstrate how to use an oxygen mask with the grace of a synchronized swimmer.

By now I don't even try to order. I stand at the counter, just another mute Japanese, and in a second a drink is plopped in front of me. I lean over the wineglass and rest my head in my hands. *She never loved her husband even though he worked for Mitsubishi bank but she was faithful to him. Rest in Peace.*

"Drink up," a voice tells me. "We're about to go." His hand is on my neck. It's the handsome man.

To show off I take a gulp that involves two large swallows. But I don't turn around. I don't want it acknowledged that it's true, that I'm actually following them.

"Wait a minute," he says. "Freda's going to the bathroom. You've got a couple of minutes. *Two more wines,*" he calls to the bartender. He finishes it off while Freda's still in line, then waits for me to do the same.

"Hits the spot," he says. "But it's a dark night for this little troupe of merrymakers. None of us will ever be the same. Each of us, in one way or the other, will be changed irrevocably. Jesus, it's hard to say that word after a few drinks. Maybe we won't even know it, but we will be. Changed, that is."

I wait politely for him to continue.

"You don't have to bow," he says.

I clear my throat. My heart is thumping. "He was your good friend?" I ask nervously.

The handsome man nods.

At a loss for what else to say I blurt out, "And he had a good job?"

"The best," he says. "You're bowing again."

"I'm sorry."

"So tell me," he begins. "What are your talents? Because each of our merrymakers has a specialty and we need to know how to slot you in. I don't suppose you sky-dive and compose New Age bird calls on a synthesizer? Because as of Tuesday, we're missing a musical sky-diver."

What are my talents? I can play the oxygen mask like a trombone. I can say in English, *The temperature in Chicago is fifty-three degrees* without making any of the American passengers burst out laughing.

"Woop. Come on," he says. "Time to go."

We're walking again, but I can hardly hold myself up. I find a wall and collapse against it. Then a street sign appeals to me. I grab onto it. It's the only thing that can rescue me from the ground. I look up to check in which direction they're heading. But they're not off to another bar. They've congregated at a fountain in the square.

One of the men holds a bottle of wine upside down over the fountain. He saves a gulp for himself, then finishes pouring. "For you, honey," Freda weeps. From her tapestry handbag she pulls out the brass canister and hands it to the other woman. "Open him up for me."

As they pour him into the fountain they produce a second bottle of wine and pass it around. The handsome man is right there at the fountain with the rest of them. This man I have seen half-naked, muscular as the statues girdling the fountain, is on all fours lapping at the water. His head hangs between his shoulders.

"Hey," says one of the men. "Come on now."

I drop my hands from the iron stake of the street sign and stand unsupported. After a moment of weaving I steady myself and then shuffle toward the fountain. In another second I'm there beside him, on all fours myself, to offer him comfort. My head drops into the water and it is only someone's hand grabbing my hair that pulls me out of it. The handsome man's fingers stroke my face clean.

"Well," one of the men remarks, helping to wipe away the ashes under my chin, "he gets around."

"He always did," says Freda.

The handsome man begins to weep. I put my arm around him.

"You loved him too," the handsome man weeps to me. "You loved him, didn't you?"

"Yes," I tell him. "I loved him." I discover this small belief. I say hello to the stranger I find under the water. Tomorrow, Singapore.

Prix Fixe

MILLER RETURNED TO SOUTHERN OHIO in time to offer some help and kindness to his failing parents. After their deaths he found a place in the woods to live and a job as chef in the dining facilities of a state park. Often in the morning he drove a long hour or more to the markets in the city, there to behold what would determine the day's special. With the crates of fresh selections snuggled into his station wagon, his thoughts on the ride back confronted the culinary equivalent of the writer's blank page. Sometimes his head swirled with exciting ideas; other mornings he was in a panic upon returning with the same old eggplant and squash and zucchini and nothing but the dullness of the word *ratatouille* standing by to mock him.

He lived right on the grounds of the state park, preferring its protected forest to the reality of the nearby Ohio hamlet, an impoverished coal town left for dead years before. Each evening he retired to his cabin where he savored a bottle of good wine and watched TV and sometimes wrote in his journal. The wine he drank never affected him. He had studied under Michel Guérard and Roger Vergé and lived in Paris for many years before getting his own restaurant in Lyons — he had never been the least conscious of his consumption until moving back to the States, where any repeated tropism passed for addiction. Now, like an alcoholic, he drank in secret exactly so people wouldn't think he was an alcoholic. He always woke up early, thirsty for water and orange juice.

On this day he was up before dawn. A sales gathering of thirty or thirty-five success stories was expected at the lodge for the weekend. Miller stood outside his cabin and waited to see if any hunters would show up. He dipped pieces of a stale baguette into his bowl of coffee and watched the fog turn the sunrise into a magician's trick.

He was happy to see Parlon Dieter's truck turning up the dirt path toward his cabin. He went inside and poured a second bowl of coffee, tore off half a baguette, and carried out a tub of butter.

Parlon Dieter was around sixty, big and strong, with a full head of barely graying hair matted down by his hunting cap. In the back of his pickup were six rabbits, a deer already dressed, and a single duck. Miller knew without asking that the deer was two weeks dead. They both agreed the extra week took out the gaminess. The other hunters could barely wait the seven days, and the deer tasted of their brutish rush. Dieter's patience paid off, and now Miller bought his venison only from him. He briefly checked over the kill and gave a buyer's nod even though he would be lucky to move a single rabbit. He wished he could serve venison to the crowd of successful pacesetters, but they were suburbanites working for an insurance company and he had already ordered dozens of Cornish hens, pre-stuffed, all of them in a row exactly alike.

Parlon Dieter accepted the bread and bowl of coffee with a polite thanks. His bare hands, sealed thick with callouses, acted as their own set of protective gloves. Dieter's wife June had the same kind of hands. She worked for Miller in the lodge, chopping and cooking in the kitchen, and often Dieter stood by and watched her, the admiration on his face. He was a shy man whose natural good manners overcame a mountain man taciturnity. With each visit to the cabin he stuttered out a tiny chapter from his life as if this were the payment required for the coffee and bread Miller had waiting for him.

The two of them stared into the distance as they slurped up their bowls. They were up on a crest and they could see the length of rising and falling woods extending to the horizon. Miller's cabin was hidden and alone, away from the ones rented on a weekly basis by budget-minded families, Ohioans for the most part who had grown up without an ocean and contentedly boated on a man-made lake. These were the people he cooked for in the summer, vacationers who wanted a tuna melt for lunch and breaded chicken for dinner. As for his chef specials, venison in traditional brown sauce, duck quenelles and shiitake mushrooms, or stuffed rabbit with chanterelle cream sauce, it was only because he bought the meat cheap from the hunters that his budget could allow it.

The sunrise had burned off most of the fog except in the hollows. Down there Parlon Dieter hunted ruffled grouse, rabbit, wild turkey, deer, and squirrel. Dieter confirmed the rumors of bobcat returning, and he told Miller that in recent weeks bald eagles had been spotted on the high rocky knobs to the north. "Seen a couple bald eagles tumbling in the air as a boy," Dieter said, "lovebirds spinning themselves into a wheel."

Then Dieter fell silent. He held his bowl of coffee with both hands, as a potter might, and stared down into the dark liquid.

"That was a sight," Miller finally said.

"It was," Dieter agreed. "My dad was with me. Wanted ever after to see it again."

Miller enjoyed listening to Parlon Dieter talk. He enjoyed the way the words had to push through his big man shyness. He liked the way Parlon Dieter accepted his coffee French style and drank it like a Frenchman.

After another long silence during which Miller considered sharing something from his own life, perhaps his wild boar anecdote, Parlon Dieter said, "Haven't told you much about my dad. Save that for later I guess."

Dieter noticeably relaxed. He seemed relieved to know what chapter he would be required to narrate next visit. Maybe then Miller would tell him about the wild boar splayed across the sidewalk. The boar lay in front of a restaurant in a village in the Ardennes, a chocolate swirl of blood issuing from its mouth. Had Miller not been a young chef's apprentice at the time with a still rudimentary grasp of the French language, he would have marched in and asked for the honor of designing a recipe for this beast at their doorstep.

He had traveled to the Belgian village with a companion of his, a struggling fellow apprentice from Yugoslavia. The dead boar sparked their hike the next day with an unknown excitement. Immersed as he and Goran were in culinary techniques, the tangled black magnificence of the Ardennes woods seemed another version of the dark forces and grand complications at work in a several course French meal. The trees, dramatically bullet-scarred from World War II, were known to jam the teeth of buzz saws with all their ingested metal. His struggling, bewildered friend from Yugoslavia reminded Miller of those fatal childhood tales woven in forests like these. Goran's talent was not strong enough to lead him out of the thicket, although for Miller the forest, as well as cuisine, easily parted into its separate ingredients. It was Miller's temperament to know all the trees, to recognize with as much effort as two plus two equals four the birch, beech, oaks, and aspen. As soon as he realized that Goran could barely distinguish a contrast between pine and hardwood, an obtuseness that in the kitchen would translate to likening cumin to cinnamon, his throat tightened with foreboding. With three years' passing, Goran was more than ever the lame boy trying to keep up with the piper's song. He suffered a nervous collapse and fled back to his home in Sarajevo. That had happened over twenty years ago; perhaps Goran was dead by now.

For a moment Miller forgot about Parlon Dieter standing next to him. The fog in the dark hollows of the Ohio woods, evaporating as he watched, captured the sensation breathing on him late nights, a feeling growing ever vaguer that visited sometimes when he was writing in his journal and found himself addressing an entry to his old friend.

Parlon Dieter put down his bowl on a tree stump. He stabbed the rest of the baguette into his shirt pocket and drove off in his truck to deliver the meat. The baguette poked out of the pocket like an oversized fountain pen. Miller knew the big man would need the bread for later, something to munch on to keep his shyness busy.

He took the bowls inside and laid them in the sink. He caught his own eyes distorted in the metal band as he rinsed out the coffee beaker, and was encouraged to check his reflection in the glass of the Matthew Brady photograph he had framed. Young soldiers staring out from the shell of their Civil War uniforms disappeared in the glare, and he could see only himself. Then he gave in and went into the bedroom and stood in front of the full-length mirror. He still admired himself but without the pleasure he once felt, a pleasure like too many calories. He was glad Parlon Dieter had never asked to use his bathroom where he would have spied his shelf of skin creams, and his layered presentation of towels, over-the-hill divas in their preposterous colors and staginess.

He got in his station wagon and drove to the lodge. The restaurant, the Wren's Room as it was called, was in the cornerstone of the lower floor, the one spot where the lodge extended into the mulchy beginning of forest. Because of the trees, the natural lighting was usually dreary, and the place felt damp.

The large dining area was empty except for William, a local boy around seventeen or eighteen. Promoted to head waiter, he was trying out another new arrangement of tables. The dull lighting coated the windows with silver so that the boy could watch himself while he worked. The boy's pleasure in himself was clear — he was tasting himself, his appetite growing. The first few restaurant tricks Miller had showed him had made the boy giddy as Icarus. About once a week William's father showed up and sat alone, letting his son wait on him. The father was a foundry worker who made historical markers for the whole country. He took a stated pride in the fact that the molds came from West Virginia dirt. He seemed to take equal pride in his boy and the way each week William might have a little improvement to show him, a linen napkin draped over his forearm, something that told the father his son was prospering in the job.

Miller smiled. The boy turned around, then came over to take Miller's garment bag off his hands. Miller had brought a suit and tie for later, should he decide to play host to the pacesetters. Probably not. Since sunrise, when that feeling had surprised him and a scrap of his lost companion had floated home, he had begun thinking of how to arrange his evening. Wine, to be sure, a Bordeaux; perhaps the duck Dieter had killed. His books would be arranged around him, the journal in his hand, but he would turn on the TV.

In the kitchen June Dieter was already at work on the rabbits, and there was Parlon Dieter beside her. She chatted to her husband amiably about one of her old-fashioned topics as she brought the cleaver down six times and deposited the heads in the plastic bag he held out for her. She was in her late fifties, maybe even sixty by now. Her hair was corded with gray. She wore it long, tied back in a thick mane.

The baguette was still poking out of Dieter's pocket. As soon as Miller walked through the door, Dieter reached for it.

"Want these heads?" June Dieter yelled over.

"No. Take them."

"Brought you some thyme and basil and cilantro from my garden."

"Good," Miller said.

"What are you going to do with these rabbits?" She didn't mind asking questions one after the other if there were answers to be had. Her voice was always on the loud side, and smartened with the whipcrack of Christian cheer. She was the best there was at dressing and butchering game.

She asked, "You doing the special with the chanterelle sauce? Parlon sure likes it."

Parlon Dieter pulled out the baguette and clamped his mouth on it.

"I don't know yet."

She wiped her hands on her apron and turned to face him. "Samson Meats'll be here at ten with the Cornish hens."

Miller said, "Will they bring them to us frozen or defrosted?"

"Good question." June Dieter strode to the kitchen door and pushed it open. The door swung back and forth. "William!" she called through the swish, the cleaver slapping against her thigh.

The boy rushed in as if June Dieter had blasted her coach's whistle. Miller moved over to his counter, the counter where he created, and studied the row of herbs and oils. He picked up the thyme Dieter's wife had laid there and pressed it against his nose and face. He pulled down the garlic. Already he was finding his way. He almost knew what to do with the rabbit. He would know in a little while.

He glanced over at William, who was stuttering out a response to June Dieter. He felt a surge of unwanted power over the boy. He would have to school him in the intangibles. First was to remove nervousness from body language. Nervousness made people feel their control over you and that was deadly for a chef. The diner should feel privileged, delightedly helpless, and always a little afraid.

He knew William had grand plans, plans to escape this town, this state, plans to be a European chef. He didn't even have to ask. It was there in the boy's looks, the suppressed yearning of his slenderness, the quivering elfin miserableness of his features upon making any mistake. Now William couldn't answer June Dieter's question, and his terror showed. He didn't know if the Cornish hens would arrive defrosted or frozen, even though he had taken the message. Two blooms of red fired up his cheeks. Miller heard the rip in June Dieter's voice. It was this ability to summon fervor that made her a leader. He had discovered her making beds in the lodge, and oh what a find: her rough face had discharged an energy commanding Miller to put a butcher knife in her hand.

"Somebody just came in and ordered pancakes," William added, blanching behind his bright flush. Under June Dieter's stare, William's face ebbed and throbbed with discoloration. It was June Dieter, not Parlon, who had told Miller about the son they had lost to leukemia and how the six grandchildren their two daughters had given them made her confront her one great hell-bound sin: an inability to love those six enough to make up for the one she had lost.

"We're not making pancakes," she told William. "We're too busy, and where's Ada?" She moved to the kitchen door and looked out. "Oh it's just Henry and Lorraine out there. Parlon, crack a few eggs on the grill. They're getting eggs and toast this morning."

William's face twisted. "You tell them," he said.

"Out! before this cleaver finds your head."

It was cartoonish the way the kitchen door fanned the wind in their faces, so quickly did William depart. Miller knew the son June Dieter had lost had been about William's age. He could see her fighting against the kind of calculations a God-fearing person should not make.

Parlon Dieter began cracking eggs into a bowl. The big, strong man tapped the shell ever so timidly, turning the egg with each tap to check for a break, then using both hands to pry the halves apart.

He did that six times, and the clumsy innocence of the sight was as pleasurable to Miller as watching the finest chef at work.

June Dieter moved in to help her husband. Her laborer's hand swelled atop the spatula Dieter was holding. She guided his even bigger, crustier hand, digging into it like prey, and forced out the energy and confidence. Together they stabbed at the eggs, then shoved them onto a plate. She flung her iron-colored ponytail over her shoulder with what appeared to be flirtatiousness, for Dieter was watching her closely, his hand released to hang powerfully dead by his side, kicked open the door, and delivered the breakfast plates herself. She left no doubt about whose hands had guided whose when they had first learned to love each other — and now, lesson given and lesson received, it was easy to picture them pawing each other in bed, something unbearably forceful and close to non-Christian in their tussling.

After delivering the eggs to Henry and Lorraine, June Dieter sat down to chat with them. The boy William jerked with some confusion at the sight and went back to arranging chairs.

Miller took a handful of thyme and began wandering. He went into the dining room and walked its far length, away from the two diners. The floor-to-ceiling windows returned his reflection. Outdoors and indoors merged so that he appeared to be impaling himself on branches as he paced. He paused for a moment at the large stone fireplace. He was standing in the Hansel and Gretel corner, or so he called it. The trees created the illusion of living deep in the forest, when in fact twenty feet away in the other direction the mowed grass and masonried landscaping began. An all-cement porch, some unbrellaed tables overlooking a wedge of man-made lake, tried its Ohio best for the Côte d'Azur effect.

Yesterday or the day before June Dieter had brought in some corn fritters and they were good, though he had limited himself to one, and now he was thinking of having her fry up the same batter but as a type of burrito, an upright sheath to hold and display the rabbit stuffing he would create.

He pressed the herb to his nose. Thyme. He loved the name and the smell. He looked out the window at the illusion of deep woods. His face too was out there, hung on a tree and returning his gaze. He drew close to the glass to lose the mirror effect. Outside, the forest panted its beefy halitus; the soil held the breaths of gloom in its dampness. Fifteen thousand years ago a glacier had sliced through this park he was living in, bringing with it the nutrients from all its travels. Fifteen thousand years ago human beings were the fable that frightened the dark woods.

"June," Miller said, a soft declarative sentence, hardly meant to be overheard, but in a second June Dieter was up from the table and there by his side. He didn't understand how it was that people became important to you. His parents, too late, were important to him. They had brought their peculiar boy into the world and tried their best, though he had taken too long to understand this and the love he had for them at the end was in fact a nostalgia for the love he should have had all along. Then there was Goran, their relationship literally forged word by word as they studied French and learned a common language together. And now in a different way was this woman June Dieter, whom he had found making beds in her white uniform, the frilly short-sleeve cuffs absurdly girlish against her bread-kneading forearms. And her long grey ponytail — ridiculous of course, except when it worked and became not ridiculous at all. June Dieter had taken a youthful braid, an aging face, and confidently served up the mutually exclusive with Appalachian zest. It was what he had tried to do in cuisine, elevating the unlikely and demeaned into an artful collaboration. It was where he had once succeeded, but not for awhile, not for a long time.

They say a great chef is great for only eight to ten years and he had lasted eleven, and no one was sorry to see him go.

And so for the people who would never ask why such a man as he was here, the vacationers with their beers and hoagies, mostly avoiding the restaurant and eating out of coolers or cooking in their own cabins, for those Ohioans or insurance company pacesetters who would never ask why a once nearly famous chef had come to a place that made a joke of who he really was, he could answer them: he was washed up.

The pacesetters sat in two long rows at the banquet tables and they looked alike, every one of them. The occasional female head or Asian black crewcut or latté skin was an illustrator's trick to hide the exactly repeated pen strokes. The people were drawn all the same, positioned shoulder to shoulder.

"This puts the death in death row," Miller said to June Dieter. They watched from the kitchen. June Dieter had stayed late to do the cooking, and Miller was padding her timecard to make sure she was well-rewarded. He hoped she didn't notice that the signs of life she had tried to breathe into the pre-fab meal were completely lost on the nouveau-executives. They gave him a bad feeling, these success stories all in a row.

He put on his coat to leave. He didn't care if they were satisfied diners. They didn't have the dimension to like or dislike his food. Rubbery baby carrots and a baked potato were just their speed, a dead and buried geometry to go with the Cornish hens. Yet June Dieter, good Christian, (becoming an aesthete too?), had tried for more: she'd whipped up bowls and bowls of garlic mashed potatoes and carefully seared fresh asparagus. William served each pacesetter individually, exhilarated by the stylish flair he could bring to spooning out gobs of starch. Then he poured them wine Miller wouldn't use for mouthwash.

"I'm leaving," Miller said. He gave up on the three rabbit loins roasting in the oven; he had three more rabbits and he could experiment again tomorrow. "I guess it's Parlon's lucky night. Thirty minutes more on those loins."

June Dieter's eyes roamed over him a bit roughly. She studied him. "All right," she said.

Although the dining hall had been closed for the banquet, a man had slipped in and now sat alone at a table by the fireplace. He seemed patiently entertained by the banquet's doings and especially by the pomp and flitting-about of William. The man's presence had lit the boy's panic flairs. Ada, who had finally arrived, and the two other night servers, Geri and Willa, coped with the unwanted diner by pretending he wasn't there.

The man wore an Ohio state parks sweatshirt — *Ohio, the heart of it all!* — the same design as the one on display in the gift shop. A ruse, Miller spotted instantly. The man's smile was too close to an ironic sneer. The haircut revealed a demand for style. His skin had been looked after. Then the man brought out a book, and Miller knew. He was vain, arranging his image even when no one was looking, playing his own little jokes with the sweatshirt. A man of the world, or at least not of this Wren's Room world.

Drawing closer, Miller glimpsed the manicured hands, the clipped and cleaned nails, and on his wrist the expensive diver's watch masquerading as a budget Timex. His hair had been colored, expertly so, but colored.

"You're being ignored. I apologize," Miller said.

"Excuse me!" the man called to William. "What's the chef's special?"

Miller allowed him this. They had looked each other in the eye, but the man still held Miller as a functionary.

"He must be a local boy." The man shook his head.

"I'm sorry, technically we're closed for a business banquet, but yes, yes of course, we don't get our help from summering gentry."

"That explains the manners or lack thereof. You, excuse me!"

he called again. He feigned (quite well) condescension, but clearly the man was taken aback by William's slender good looks, a prettiness that went completely unnoticed against the burly, rifle rack aesthetic favored in this region. Clearly the man was aware that Miller understood the subtle arching of eyebrows. It appeared almost to be staged for his benefit.

To a scurrying, nearly distraught William the man said, "Can you find your way clear to wait on me this evening?"

William stood at the edge of the man's table, gulping breaths. The man watched him, loving it.

"I'm your waiter, sir. My name is William."

"William, I'm struck by your accent. What town are you from? I'm getting a strong feeling you're from Homer or Gomer or Claysville."

Miller's annoyance swelled into anger, but he knew the expression on his face remained calm, even serene. He was glad the boy was wise enough not to answer, to retreat into polite bewilderment.

"So what's the chef's special?" the man asked.

"Rabbit," Miller told him.

"I'll try it," the man said. He opened his book, *Dante's Inferno.*

"An appetizer, sir?"

"You have appetizers here?"

"I can make one, if you'd like," Miller said.

The man went back to his book. "No thank you. I'll settle for terza rima as my prologue."

Miller went back into the kitchen. He opened the refrigerator. In a bowl was the corn fritter batter June had stirred up and he had thinned out. Next to it was the rabbit saddle marinating in a puddle of lemon juice, garlic, and the fresh thyme from her garden. Too obvious, he thought. Such predictable seasonings. Already he saw the man's amused sneer.

"You're back," June Dieter said.

"Yes." He pressed his palms against the counter. He tried to muscle the shaking from his hands. He pressed harder. Obvious seasonings, perhaps, but no more obvious than *Dante's Inferno*. God no.

"Are you all right?" June Dieter had come up behind him. Her hands dug into his shoulders. Such strength, Miller thought. For a moment he leaned back into her care.

"Just tell me what you want me to do," she said.

William burst in, panicking over the pacesetters' dessert.

"We're busy!" June Dieter hollered. "Do it yourself!"

The pieces of cake were already Saran-wrapped on individual plates. William grabbed at them and began stacking them up his arm.

"Just put them on a tray!" June Dieter yelled.

William's arm snapped and sent three plates to the floor. His features struggled to remain composed. June Dieter drove an Old Testament warning into her mighty sigh, then turned her back on him.

Miller looked at the boy's crumbling face. Goran, he thought, surprised he hadn't seen it before. He pulled shallots and cilantro and garlic onto the counter. Where was Goran now? The carrots were fresh and tangy; he pulled them down. Dead? He asked June Dieter to mince the rabbit saddle and garlic and shallots and cut the carrots into minuscule cubes. The wine he needed, Bordeaux, a 1989 French Talbot, was in his private, locked stock. As he fished out his keys, he asked June Dieter to go outside and break him off a juniper sprig. As he had hoped, Parlon got up to do it for her. He still needed June to help him.

He was working like a fast-order cook, and he liked the way that felt, braising the marinated saddle with some cinnamon and morita chiles, then adding the shallots, garlic and carrots to create a stuffing.

June Dieter sliced the kidney, fried it and mixed it with some cabbage and porcini mushrooms to sculpt a small mound of salad on the plate.

He poured a dipperful of corn fritter batter on the grill, smoothed it into a bumpy crepe, turned it at its first browning and laid the stuffing in. The corn fritter crepe was a little stiff; he had to be careful not to crack it as he rolled it into a burrito. He cut the burrito at a sharp diagonal and arranged it one half standing up in a stiff spike, the other half fallen.

On the white space still left on the plate he poured tears of haberno pepper oil and dropped eyes of cilantro oil into then. He grabbed the fire-hot rabbit loin from the oven and placed it over the eyeball tears of oil. The plate immediately burst with an exotic heat. He took the juniper sprig and crushed it on top.

His shoulders rumbled with the train running through his body, but inside his head it was quiet. He looked up to find June Dieter and William, standing as two soldiers, attentive to his next command. "Do it right," he said, pushing the bottle of Bordeaux to William. "You understand that he's trying to disrupt you?"

William swallowed hard.

"You understand that you must stay composed?"

"Do you understand that if you don't stay composed I'm going to slap you upside your head!" June Dieter warned.

Miller drew close to William, lips to ear. His whisper was close to a hiss. "You goddam hillbilly, how are you going to get out of here if you can't conquer one smart-ass diner?"

William compressed his mouth, his nose, his rapidly blinking eyes. Perhaps there was hope for him after all, as there never was, really, for Goran.

After William left, Miller went over to the sink and washed his shaking hands. June Dieter came over. She had a plate in her hand and was spearing a fork into the burrito scrap.

"Don't do it," he asked. "Don't reassure me."

"It's delicious," she said.

"Don't." He closed his eyes, still leaning on the counter.

Most of the pacesetters were gone now, causing a sudden pressure drop into stillness. A few remained, chatting over coffee and wine. The last straggles of tinkling cups settled over Miller.

Sitting on a stool, his dinner plate on a wooden chopping block, Parlon Dieter hunched over the other braised rabbits. "Parlon, tell the man how much you like those rabbits," June Dieter instructed.

Parlon didn't say anything, but he nodded. Sometimes Miller conjured pictures, he couldn't help it, it was Parlon Dieter's own stolidness that compelled him, of what that face would look like disfigured in love-making. The spread of pounded features —-soft broken nose, a razor slice of eyes, cinder lips — he saw June Dieter taking him further, to the point that pain and pleasure broke apart his poker face. Miller himself sometimes wanted to love June Dieter, that young hair, that old face, he wanted to grab and smother those two worlds.

William rushed back in. "That guy wants a word with you," he said, pulling down another wine glass.

"How can you get out of breath running but ten feet?" June Dieter demanded.

"And I think he's rich," William gasped.

Miller glanced toward the wine glass. "What's that for? he asked.

"He wants you to join him."

"Please tell him I've left."

"But he saw you," William said. "He knows you're here."

"You heard him," June Dieter snapped. "Elvis has left the building, boy! Do I have to go out there and tell him myself."

"Yes, do," Miller said. "You join him. Why don't you. The meal is half yours."

June narrowed her eyes at him. He saw her frisky defiance. God, he thought, if only she'd gotten out of the holler at an earlier age.

"And what exactly should I say?" June Dieter asked.

"Say, Monsieur is disappointed? Perhaps he was hoping for a duck magret in persimmon and Armagnac sauce?"

"Well, I'll just say *Monsieur*," she said. "I'll say I hope Monsieur is enjoying the meal. I will," she said. "I'll say it." Then she strode out.

Parlon got up from his stool and, still chewing, watched out the window of the swinging door. "Sitting down," he reported. "And she ain't being asked to leave."

"Did he mind his manners?" Parlon Dieter asked in his sincere, wooden fashion after his wife showed up very late at Miller's cabin. The two of them were sitting outside. Encircled by mosquito torches, he and Dieter looked to be part of a sacrificial ritual.

June Dieter pulled a chair into their protected circle. "Oh Parlon honey, that man wants a woman as much I want a fly in my soup."

Miller went inside his cabin to retrieve another bottle of wine. Across the room the glass of the Matthew Brady photograph reflected his image. He found his face among the young soldiers, the same stare but no longer one of them; instead, their father.

June Dieter was telling her husband, "Good gracious, Parlon, where's your eyes? Honey, it wasn't me he was after. I was nothing but a bodyguard for that poor little boy."

"Who are we talking about?" Miller asked, though he knew.

"Parlon, you're a hunter and you know about predators and their prey and by God I'm not explaining it any further to you."

"What happened?" Miller asked.

"Nothing happened. I didn't leave until that boy was safe and sound inside his car, I made sure of that."

"It wouldn't take nothing to follow him."

"My lord, Parlon," she said. "I can only do so much."

Miller opened the wine with a corkscrew. He found himself mimicking William's theatrical nervousness and flair, and was glad the torch flames distorted everything.

"That boy's too young to know his own secrets," June Dieter declared.

"He's young, he's got time," Miller said and instantly regretted it. He poured Dieter another glass, then asked, "So you seen any bobcat lately?"

"Oh yeah, I seen 'em."

There was a long pause, long enough for the woods to grow noisy around the hollow of their silence, and Miller could feel June Dieter's muscles ready themselves to jump in and save the conversation.

Then Parlon Dieter said, "When I'm hunting I picture my son stepping out from behind a tree. I pick out the tree and sit down and wait for him."

Even June Dieter met these words with a startled shiver.

Miller thought, I should say something. I should make a move. And he thought, I can't.

Goran had struggled three years before giving up — as giving up he should. He had no talent. Miller should have told him. He should have helped to redirect him instead of encouraging a dream he knew would be broken. But then Goran might have left, and he wanted Goran there for him as he rose to success, not that he could give Goran much attention during the ascent. But for the best people in love, love had to wait for them to become the best — how easy to proclaim that when you were young. How easy to say good-bye when they decide not to wait for you.

He could hear the blood striking his temples. Beat, beat, beat.

"A barred owl," Parlon said and got up from his chair. He walked over to the edge of woods.

June reached down for the wine. Miller took the bottle and poured it for her. "Your husband needs you," he told her.

"Parlon works out things in his own way." She reached over in the dark and took hold of his hand. "Don't worry about William," she said. "He'll be all right."

Furgus Welcomes You

ANGELA DAHLGREN WAS THE FIRST to hear it. The sound wasn't thunderous and it wasn't messy — that was something she could have handled. Her family had once been a lot bigger and a lot noisier; it was all thunder and mess, and that was what she was used to. The women had kept the volume loud and steady; the men threw in a moo from time to time. They were farmers or not farmers, that's how they thought of themselves, in terms of farming, and the farming was in their voices — low and earthy efforts at sounds that arrived spaced apart, the words furrowed into separate rows. She used to think of the men as terribly thoughtful, plowing through a thick soil of brain matter to get to just the right syllable. Now she didn't think of them that way.

She had married into Robert's family and watched it grow and grow in membership while her own family impossibly dwindled. It was only her mother now and an unmarried older brother, a farmer, thirty-eight years old, who had recently placed a personal ad in *Farm Journal*. Sometimes during the mornings she and her mother made the long journey to McDonald's, fifty-five miles away. If it was raining, her brother tagged along, stretched out in the backseat, lonely and bleak as the Iowa weather. *Would like a pretty wife*, his ad began. The long van (the kind used by daycare centers) was otherwise empty; there was none of the excited Sunday squawking from her husband's wildly branching family about who was going to order what. In their town of Furgus, traditions were adhered to, and Sundays meant church, and after church meant McDonald's. When three generations of her in-laws were packed into the long van, tradition dictated that the eldest son inherit the driving rights. That meant Robert, Angela's husband, despite his recently broken arm. A long plaster cast imprisoned the right arm in mid-throw. Even with his limb thus crooked like an Allen wrench, he wasn't about to surrender his inheritance. The driving rights were his due, and he wasn't giving them up even if everybody's life was imperiled. Angela's father-in-law, still the hometown basketball hero at sixty eight, conceded the pilot's chair but sat shotgun as co-pilot, lording over his bequest.

During the week, though, it was just Angela and her mother and brother, the three of them vague and clinging — *flyover pathetic* was how she chose to describe their threesome, imagining the word spewed out by disgusted sophisticated East Coasters — because, yes, she read *The New Yorker*. She worried about the fumbling effect on her sons, but no, there was no worry. They would never grow up to be like her. Both of them looked just like Robert, increasing her sense of depletion. Her own genes were too faded and ghostly; they didn't stand a chance against her husband's advancing army. Her family members were like longjohns hanging emptily on the laundry line, if not sickly and wan in color, then blown away completely by death's wind. Her grandparents some years before. Her father not long after. Then her sister, just last year, her first plane ride ending in disaster.

When she heard it — that sound — she wished she hadn't, but at least it was something, something definite — finally, *something*. She was leaving Furgus with her mother and brother when the van suddenly became even more silent, as if an unnoted buzz had drawn attention to itself by switching off. Once at McDonald's her brother briefly came to life, putting away two Value Meals and telling them about some future wife who had answered his personal ad; they were meeting at a halfway point, the Dairy Bar in Larksburg. Her mother, a quart drinker of heavily-sugared coffee, triumphantly ordered the cheapest size, then held out her tiny cup for umpteen free refills. By the time she was done, lipstick and nervous chewing had left bloody toothmarks around the styrofoam rim. A castle of sugar packs toppled and poured to the floor as her mother tripped over the table on their way out. Then of course she twice needed bathroom breaks on the ride home. Since there were no rest stops or gas stations or even trees, Angela simply pulled over to the side of the road and her mother opened front and back doors and sat between them on the running board. Her brother obliged by remaining conked out on the backseat.

Angela stood by the driver's window while she waited out the second pit stop. The coffee drained slowly from the prolapsed bladder on the other side. Her mother sat on the running board, relaxed and almost luxuriating. The threat of a passing car didn't seem to bother her in the least.

As she stood waiting, Angela looked across the road and noticed bright gashes defacing the berm. She walked over to take a closer look. Two stick figures drawn in yellow spray paint abruptly rose before her. Accident victims, gruesomely inscribed on the road. She drew back, frightened, before approaching again, careful not to touch their outlines with her foot.

A terrible heaviness plunged in her chest. There was not a car in sight. How could such a thing have happened here? She remembered taking her sister to the airport. Her first plane ride — how ludicrous not to have flown dozens of times by her age. Her sister had been scared getting on the plane, but giddy too. Her sister's face, the last time Angela had seen it, so silly with joy and fear. The silly face turned right toward her, to catch her eye, and then a final wave.

Suddenly a pickup with oversized tires came storming down

the deserted road and plowed right over the painted bodies. The sadness that clenched at her was violent and she found herself doubled over, reaching out to the fender for support. She steadied herself: regular deep breaths. A long minute passed. She got back in the van and blew her nose and waited for her mother to finish. As usual, they drove the rest of the way in silence.

Ahead was the Furgus town limits, sheet metal stamped into a discolored banner waving any strays into town — *Furgus Welcomes You!* Staked next to it was a plaque that looked like a NO PARKING sign, celebrating the state basketball championship fifty-one years earlier. The still famous team had featured her father-in-law as a forward.

Furgus, a prairie town in Iowa, was small enough that hardly anyone had actually been there, yet the name Furgus sounded so familiar, familiar as that uncle tangled deep in the family tree, what's-his-name, the one always pictured with an ear trumpet lifted to his skull.

She had almost forgotten about the sound until it turned on again as she entered Furgus. As soon as the van whipped past the town boundary, a buzz grazed the silent air. It was strange. Leaving Furgus, the van had tumbled into nothingness; something noticeable had switched off. Entering Furgus, it had picked up a notch. Something had turned on, something wiry and sonic, as soon as she sliced across the town line. One two, as quick as that. She couldn't explain it because she was describing degrees of silence, but it was there, an insistent, fragile tickling trying to get inside her.

The next day in the middle of her housework she felt a ringing in her ears. It almost made her dizzy. She had to sit down. She mistook the thrumming in her head for the toxic afterlife of furniture polish combined with ammonia cleansers. She closed her eyes to rest and slept for twenty minutes. When she woke up, it had stopped. She listened carefully to make sure it was gone, yes it was gone — but then her vigilant attention intercepted it. It was back, the Furgus silence, the extra helping of quiet nothings fingering her skull. A sonic wire brushing against her hair.

She mentioned it to her boys when they came in from school. The younger one, only six, still lived the playful life of imagination and instantly agreed. His stalk of stiff yellow hair stood straight up in a cartoon of fright. Bobby, Jr., the nine-year old, the latest in a long series of Robert Dahlgrens, had already mastered his progenitors' hiccup of dismissal. He scoffed at her description of this strange noiseless noise — at his own mother he scoffed. She saw her husband and father-in-law in the way Bobby hunched his shoulders to anything in life he didn't want to hear or know about, the doors slamming inside. Pretty soon the little one would be like that, too, the curiosity gone, the imagination gone, the hiccup in place to cut things off before they started. His hair standing on end would be the last thing that reached out to the world.

But then it was the nine-year old, Bobby Jr., such a grown-up man, who came to them in the middle of the night and wanted to be held. He said something was screaming far away inside his head. He slept between them in bed. Then her husband heard it, too. He said it sounded like a high frequency channel. In the morning they called the power and light company; her husband explained that the sound was so thin and piercing it must be coming from electrical threads inside their walls. She couldn't help a moment of pleasure when the serviceman met her husband's suggestion with a loud, coughed-up airball of ridicule. Her husband's shoulders bunched higher and he walked away. *Hey, how'd he break his arm,* she wanted the serviceman to ask. *Riding his nine-year-old's kiddie bike,* she wanted to tell him. Greenstick fracture in three places, but his pride was snapped cleanly in two. She wanted to say, *And it gave me no small amount of satisfaction.*

A technician from the telephone company came next. He checked the house and the poles outside, but he found nothing amiss. He was cocky in a winning, friendly sort of way. He told her he was so good at his job he could hear a phone ringing two houses down. Like right now, he said. It's ringing. A few minutes later he said, I wish they would answer it. Ah, so you're hearing it too, she said. He left, shaking his head. As soon as he closed the door, a telephone actually began to ring — her own phone in the den. The technician's head swung this way and that, more confused than ever. He climbed inside his service truck. Judging from the smell that had rushed from him when she first opened the door, he drove straight back to the Markey Tavern.

The phone rang at least ten times, but the caller showed no signs of giving up, so she knew it was her mother. A short message concerning her brother's date in Larksburg. Success. Not such a lark after all. Already talk of marriage. Angela hung up, wondering what was wrong with her brother. She couldn't erase the image of the stricken face of her sister's fiance when her brother had filled plate after plate at the outdoor luncheon following the funeral, with each plate remembering his sister less and enjoying the food more until he raised up from a buttery corn cob and stared blankly, the dripping cob showing more life than his eyes. It was the same zero look he gave in McDonald's midway through his second Value Meal. The fiance left Furgus soon after the funeral. Her mother had channeled all her grief into anger over the way he made sure to drop out of their lives. Each December she left an empty spot right in the middle of her yarn clothesline of Christmas cards, so that his cruel negligence hung there in the air, as visible as a missing front tooth.

In her head the sound continued. Then came threats of a high wind even though the sky was clear. She covered her ears with her hands and sank down on the couch. Her stoppered ears acted as seashells; she eavesdropped on her body at work.

Her heart pumped blood in a deep, percussive invasion. The blood curled its steady message through the fanfare of veins and arteries. She listened. Her brain received the signals, then promptly scrambled them. She wished for something she could understand: A simple brick through a window. A grain elevator explosion. A clear-cut family argument at dinner, with crescendo and then peace and dessert.

She walked out of the house. Now the neighbors were hearing it, too. They came running, telling her yes, yes they could hear it, a remote, high-tension feedback. It was driving them crazy. Yes, they were hearing it, a type of whistle, a dog whistle perhaps, wound down in frequency.

Angela nodded, said she was on her way to check it out. She looked up at the sky. The wind was coming but it hadn't arrived. Again she was visited by the image of longjohns on a clothesline, the wind sending the arms and legs in a skewered dance. It was all that was left of them, her grandparents, her father, her sister, the face of her sister as she turned with her silly face to wave... The figures on the road had been painted in crime scene fashion, portraying the twisted swastika of limbs. The yellow outlines evoked the flattened bodies that must have been left after it happened. Now she remembered. Her husband's dismissive hiccup had poofed the newspaper as he read; he seemed unmoved by the story of a father and son from Council Bluffs changing a flat tire. On the road had been drawn two outlines, vastly different in size. It had barely registered when she first saw them, but now it came back. There was a big outline and a much smaller outline with a tender, baby-nosed profile. A little boy helping his dad. They were changing tires. They were paired on the road, the little one cupped and protected by his father. Why had the painter felt the need to be so graphic? Was it really necessary to include the cute little button nose? What was the lesson he was trying to hammer home? Or was he just being sadistic, using his painterly talent to impose pain?

How could such a thing have happened near Furgus, in the middle of nowhere? Nothing happened in nowhere, that was the point.

It was getting dark now. Her boys would be home from school. She was almost there. She strode toward the plaque commemorating the state basketball championship fifty-one years earlier. *Thank You For Visiting Furgus!* called out to her. Just a couple more steps. *Please Drive Carefully* offered the backside of the town limits sign. Ha, but she was walking. What homey words of wisdom did Furgus offer for the departing pedestrian?

As soon as she stepped over the town limits the sonic piercing immediately halted. Her mind stopped trembling. Her brain seemed to plop into a pool of quiet.

She made a test. She dipped a leg back over the town border — *buzz!* — then immediately pulled back — *peace.* She threw a stone at the championship plaque. Her husband's father had been on the team. A forward with a twenty-foot set shot. Still a big hero. But he had passed the reins over to his son Robert. He let him drover the wild one-armed rides to McDonald's, plaster cast and all. Her husband could hiccup at the world all he wanted, but what did the world think of him and his swollen pride behind the wheel?

She stood just beyond the Furgus town limits and watched. She could see her cute little boys waving to her as they boarded the school bus. Each day they had turned at the last moment to catch her eye, and each day she had lived all of the morning with her heart broken in joy, reliving the expression on their faces, their tiny waves. *Mommy, good-bye. Mommy, good-bye.*

That old uncle, that what's-his-name back deep in the family tree — he had lifted an ear trumpet to one ear and then the other, and received nothing in return. The world's singing had stopped for him and he had loathed it. But what a blessing, she thought. What a blessing zero can be. How simple to add or subtract. How much harder when different figures waved before you.

The buzzing had stopped. She turned around and kept walking. *Baby, good-bye. Baby, good-bye. Sister, good-bye.*

The Home Jar

MOST OF THE TRAVELERS who come through our doors are not at all like Mr. Smith. They are polite, honest, what my night manager calls decent folk, and as thoughtful of others as they can be in the midst of their purposeful lives. Guests do not come to our hotel simply to vacation. We're not located in that kind of city. They are here for some industrious function, for a state government meeting, for example, or to attend a convention. If they are here otherwise, there is usually something wrong. We recently had a couple who stayed two weeks, waiting for an organ donation for their infant daughter. In the middle of the night they were summoned by the university hospital. Carrie Mae and Rita, who took the call, tracked them down with me at the pool. This man and his wife were sitting in chairs, staring ahead at nothing. The pool made the air dense. Upon hearing the news of the hospital's summons, the husky face of the mother, pocked with deadly worry, suddenly lit up with delight. The effect, quite honestly, was frightful. All of our hotel staff emptied onto the street, weeping, almost everyone weeping, and waving good-luck. The taxi sped off to the fanfare awaiting at the hospital.

In the glare of the couple's elated faces no one else saw the darker energy running quite apart from anxiety for their dying daughter. It was something I recognized from my own eluding of danger and tragedy: behind the brain's curtain runs a pleasure that is against your own will. This man and his wife, they were overweight, country folk. No one had ever listened to them before. They were relishing the sense of their own importance. They were enjoying the show that for once in their lives was all about them. It was the same feeling I had leaving my country, my wife, my two children. My face grew old in a week's passage under the weight of so many conflicting emotions, yet each time I handed over my passport or had my baggage sniffed by dogs and then fingered item by item before my eyes, or was asked to wait against a wall, I considered all the money and endless logistics and international agreements that enforced these precautions and it was as if the whole world was for a moment focused solely on me. That was a sensation I liked and only by pressing myself hard against the wall could I tamp down what threatened to become a smile. Yet even with my poker face the officials must have sensed some wayward emotion, for I was stopped and questioned and searched time and time again. I could well relate to these young confused parents, even though they were American, white, fed overly much but not fed well at all, even though they had never heard of my nation, even though they were no more than TV-watchers who had been pulled from their favorite programs to deal with a tragedy. They were like so many others, in the great cities of the world or in my messy village — average, complacent people with no great thoughts and no reason to think them, for whom comes a violent knock on the door that will drive them to ruin or to triumph.

Mr. Smith, however, is nothing like this couple, and Mr. Smith is what I'm here to talk about. Nor is he anything like our other guests. During his latest trip to Ohio it fell upon me to attend to him. I brought his luggage up to his room and laid out the big rectangular suitcase on the rack. It was and is hard for me to tell the ages of Americans, but I can tell you his appearance. He was tanned, and the vertical line scoring each side of his jaw was something in America that would make him handsome. It was carved there through hard work in the gym, not by the hard work of just existing in some wretched place without sunscreen. Mr. Smith was wearing a gray crew-neck sweater. Across the chest of the sweater was threaded a colorful EKG. A maroon design spiked up and down, duplicated by a turquoise line pulsing underneath. I couldn't help but think of the man (and his heavy, pock-marked wife) who had departed just a few hours earlier, so carelessly beefy where Mr. Smith was trim, so simple in their emotions — grief/ hope — where he was calibrated (even then, that was already my impression). Mr. Smith wore khaki pants. His shoes looked as comfortable as slippers. They were soft leather with rubbery soles. What called the most attention to him was his hair. It was longish and cut in one length and it was brushed back as if by the wind. It was also unusually yellow. So that is what he looked like. He wasn't young, but like I said, I couldn't guess his age beyond that.

After finishing with his suitcase, I checked the bedside lamps, tested the hair dryer, jiggled the toilet handle. I paused in the bathroom for a few extra seconds. There was something there: a vague smell of chlorine. When I breathed it in, that man and his wife sprang to life again, sitting in the pool area in the middle of the night, some other presence in the thick odorous air. Catching myself, I jerked back to my duties and quickly made my way to the door.

Although I am grateful for them, I still find it embarrassing to receive tips. Mr. Smith stopped me. "Ho there." He fished in his pockets and came up empty. "Wait," he said when my hand reached again for the doorknob.

Now he had flipped open the suitcase I had laid out for him and was checking under the folded layers of his clothes. "You guys turn on all the lights to buy time, don't you?"

My first impulse was to make a mental note of the phrase 'to buy time' so I could absorb it later. I thought of and kept to myself a remark I might have made about the importance in this case of making sure the hair dryer worked for the sake of his beautiful hair. I could have made the observation that peeking under carefully folded clothes for loose money seemed itself a none too subtle counterfeit, and at precisely the same moment as these possibilities played out (the workings of the brain fascinate me — for example, thinking of that rural couple praying in the hospital, for I knew they would be praying, while simultaneously finding myself fascinated by Mr. Smith's appearance) I understood what he was saying — that turning on the lights was a way to play indigent.

Mr. Smith was accusing me.

"I am not a beggar, Mr. Smith."

"You know my name." He turned around with a vivid smile, an outsized reaction that did not match in tone my remark to him or his simple reply to me. I had become aware that the name Smith was just like Tesfai, the most common of names at home. My own name, in fact, was Tesfai. I thought of my wife and two daughters, how they were named exactly as so many others, so many thousands upon thousands as to make them less than one. I could go days without thinking about them even while everything I did, every minute I worked, every dollar and quarter I shoved into an old jar, was devoted to them. My nephew, who lived with me, thought nothing of raiding this jar for his own pleasure until I took a stick to him and beat at him with all my might, chasing him from apartment to hallway to stairwell to backyard, a crowd swelling behind us. It was just the two of us in a one-bedroom apartment near the airport. I slept on the couch so that he could have his indulgence of a private room. I had given him all this. I was not going to let him steal from me. The cheering crowd seemed to agree with me.

Mr. Smith continued to fish in his suitcase. This time I opened the door and stepped out. He followed me into the hall and clasped my forearm to pull me back in. "I'm getting there," he said.

I said nothing although my mind was racing. When I say something I think it should be well-phrased and well-enunciated — and, for example, I hate the way my nephew has begun to mutter at me, especially as I have given up my room for him, especially as I more often than not use the kitchen sink for shaving and brushing my teeth. He has begun going out with boys other than Eritreans, not the Somalis but the Americans, black boys who couldn't look or act more dissimilar. They are big where he is not, variantly colored and featured, and rude. Yet to other Americans' sharpless eyes, Lucas is not differentiated, so this is something new I have to worry about, the fact that Lucas will be taken for an American black. Each night after school he goes directly from the school bus to the library, where I pick him up after work. He is in the eighth grade and has recently turned fourteen. No one knows he isn't my son. At the library I've watched him there, at the computers with his group of comrades, a fatherless boy who seems too happy with his friends. His mother didn't live long enough to teach him manners that would stick. He has started thrusting his hands across his face and chest when he speaks, and when I tell him to stop he switches to English and turns that language into a terrible mumbling sound. From behind a pillar I've observed a librarian scuttle over and admonish his group when they're too loud, almost yelling at each other, their hands all doing a dance. Lucas looks up at the librarian with eyes so dark they glisten as to become their opposite, white diamonds. He glows with beauty, yet what comes out of his mouth is slack and dirty as coal. And when the librarian leaves, he and his group are silent but holding back grenades of laughter. This seems sinful in light of the fact that I watched his father die (which I know is unfair, as if Lucas should live his life sadly, his father never leaving his thoughts). At the international clinic the pattern of my brother's heart loped across the screen, vibrantly patterned exactly as that imprint upon

Mr. Smith's sweater, the maroon and turquoise threads of health and happiness and wisdom, all the things we came to America to search for. And now my nephew has health. And he'll have wealth if he starts stealing from others the way he has started to steal from me. And he has happiness with his friends — too much so, his happiness like the fumes of gasoline.

So you can see that receiving a tip prompts in me an unreasonable bout of hapless mental wanderings. Carrie Mae and Rita tell me to just say thank you, honey (a compelling idea until I realized the honey was directed at me) but just as we don't match as people, what words we use cannot match either. Carrie Mae and Rita can keep themselves awake through their shift by laughing all night as if their impossibly big chests are fueled with an eight-hour supply of caffeinated guffaws. They can say thank you, honey, and it would work because American black women with impossibly big chests can say that; people like them to say it.

Mr. Smith said, "You got it down, don't you, man?" That seemed unfair since I had already once made my departure, since it was he who had pulled me back from the corridor. The phrase I had practiced in my head died in my throat. Mr. Smith had seemed someone equal to my tangled politesse, someone who wouldn't think it absurd to trade formalities with me. He handed over two dollars. And what did I say? Nothing. But I did tuck my head into a bow, and I heard from him a dry cough, which I interpreted as a chuckle.

That evening I was working an extra shift when Mr. Smith left for dinner. I was there to take his parking ticket. I had been getting extra work as the parking attendant ever since three employees had been fired for overcharging. The line of waiting cars extended into the abyss of the parking garage. There had been a rape here two months earlier, somewhere back in those dark recesses, yet none of us, including the women, thought of this as a dangerous job. The garage was open twenty-four hours a day, and even Fawzia, an astonishingly beautiful Somali girl who often did the night shift, had met no trouble.

The face behind the windshield of the third car was erased by the cavernous shadow, but I could see the glow of Mr. Smith's yellow mane.

I had some trouble getting the time clock to accept his ticket. I wondered if he thought I was stalling. It was as if we had a great deal of history between us, yet all that was between us were a few lines of English and of course the cauldron of crisscrossing thoughts I had poured into those few lines. Had those thoughts been expressed we would have had a relationship, perhaps a friendship. But that had not happened. The time clock finally punched out its tally.

"That's a hefty fee," he said. Well, there was another word for me to write down. Mr. Smith, disconcerting as he was, was good for my education. I enjoyed the visitors most who could teach me new words. Sadly, I hadn't learned a thing in two weeks from the young couple with the dying infant. They had been satellited from the hospital to a talk show that very morning and we had all watched. The university hospital had performed a multiple organ transplant among three infants, two living, one a donor. The young couple was lumped on a couch, their bodies indistinguishable, their hands emerging from a single limb and twining together. Their voices quavered and they spoke using the vocabulary words I could no longer hear without thinking of them: God, mercy, judgment, hope, love. Carrie Mae and Rita were bouncing up and down in front of the TV, waiting to hear their own names called out and blessed on national TV, and it was strange, I too found myself anticipating right along with them and was disappointed (surprisingly so) when my name wasn't singled out for deepest gratitude. We had been their family for two weeks, night and day, we had talked of life and death issues in the most simplistic of terms but with a kind of frankness that neither of them, they told us, had experienced in their whole lives, and they marveled that this kind of intimacy and affection had happened with people who were so very different from them, the kind of people they had never met before in their small town but only heard about and about whom had formed opinions they now saw were wrong, and they had come to the conclusion that we were angels of God sent down in disguise. This profound bond we thought we had formed might have been true or might have been false — I think it was true — but in either case it was over.

"Do you gouge all your customers?" Mr. Smith's tiny car hadn't left the parking garage. His fingers still snaked inside the coin well to retrieve his credit card.

"We like to buy time, Mr. Smith." He gave no sign that he recognized me. Nevertheless I was pleased with my inside joke. I relived it as I took the bus to the library. When I got to the computer section, barely before their eight o'clock closing, Lucas was alone. He was starving. The day's tip money intended for the jar I spent on fast food, value meals supersized beyond my salary. But Lucas loved the food, and I had kept him waiting too long.

Admittedly, the people who come for conventions like to have a little fun in the midst of their business at hand, and sometimes they can get loud enough that we have to phone up to their rooms. Usually just the mildest rebuke quiets them down. Mr. Smith doesn't like noise and all of the staff know this and he is never put on any of the floors where conventioneers stay. The people here for the state legislature meetings tend to be quiet, unless they are lobbyists or the representatives themselves. We keep them on a different floor as well. But in the end, Mr. Smith requested that the rooms to either side of him be kept empty. He requested this nicely, with that smile of his that seems so at odds with what he says, and he paid for the empty rooms as well.

All this I was told by Carrie Mae and Rita. Despite their levity, they refer to the male customers as gentlemen. They stay polite about guests even when talking between themselves. Carrie Mae has five grandchildren already and one of her daughters has a drug problem and has been in jail and her two kids are going here and there because they have different fathers, one of whom is also in jail. The unjailed one doesn't want to take care of the one who is not his. Rita has a daughter who graduated from college and is a management trainee at a rental car company in Los Angeles. Her son received a partial athletic scholarship to college, a good athlete but, as she says, "not good enough to ruin his life." He's now an insurance agent at Nationwide and lives in town and often stops by. He looks good in a white shirt and tie. Carrie Mae and Rita have these conversations about their family very often. I am always worried about being asked to participate, and on this morning my fears seemed about to become justified. They called me over — just as I was about to duck away and escape. The two of them together melt into each other, and they talk like soulmates, and the differences in their children, though grave from all appearances, seem to them more like differences in the foods they prefer. That's nice for them, they are good women with expansive emotions, but the gulf between us is something they couldn't understand, the gulf itself I mean, and I don't want my family members treated like an exotic food item that with one taste can suffice their understanding. "Tesfai," they called again.

There was no avoiding them.

I needn't have worried. That "weird blond guy gentleman" I'd met yesterday was on his way to the hotel gym, they told me, and I needed to stand guard and make sure no one else entered while he did his workout. He's mister important gentleman, they laughed, and I went off to the workout room and pressed my face against the darkened glass until I could see Mr. Smith, in white shorts and a tangerine polo shirt. His chin was thrust upward as he walked the treadmill, and with his hair swept back, he looked as ever in some kind of godlike pose, even though it was the overhead TV responsible for his posture. He glanced over and saw me outside the door and signaled hello. I took this to mean he was also contentedly alone, that I needn't enter and check. His gait on the treadmill was indefinably his. I took up guard out of sight. After forty or fifty minutes I was bored enough to try to imitate Mr. Smith's gait, which I did, up and down the corridor. I had to use the restroom. Although I was quick, still I peeked through the glass to make sure no one had entered in my absence. Mr. Smith was lying on a bench, shoving barbells above his head. He put the barbells back in their rack and whipped a towel around his neck. He held on tightly to each end of the towel, his head slumped from the weight of being pulled. His body heaved heavily and I thought he might fall over. Then he straightened and shrugged his shoulders up and down and stretched his arms up high and pushed them against the wall to force them higher. His workout was over. I hurried away to ensure his privacy.

Downstairs the lobby had been thrown into chaos. A convention in town for a cheerleading competition meant that the lobby was crowded with girls dressed in their team outfits. Large duffel bags littered the floor. The parents were clothed in stretch jeans and sweatshirts. The heavier mothers had short hair with the front part curled unstylishly and all of them to me began to look alike. The men, with bellies and baseball caps, kept relifting the duffel bags whose bright thick letterings PANTHERS! WARRIORS! STRIKERS! seemed to express their own panic as fathers. I took note of the parents because they were in such contrast to their attractive cheerleading daughters. This gave me a spasm of joy. I saw the infant daughter of the young couple in the hospital. She had grown up to become beautiful, and her unbeautiful parents were overflowing with pride.

It took at least two hours to clear the lobby, directing everyone to the convention center, helping to carry down duffel bags, and making phone calls to coaches and other teammates when their cell phones gave out.

Afterwards I was sitting in a corner, ending my shift with a cup of tea, when one of the maids came down. In the preternatural quiet of the empty lobby I heard the pounce of her sneakered feet. I could see that she was upset. By now Carrie Mae and Rita had gone home and Smooshie was working the front desk. "You left your housekeeping cart?" Smooshie confronted the maid. "You need to get back up there." She picked up a ringing phone. "Go," she ordered the maid. "I'll take care of it." Distractedly she waved me over, then ignored me until she hung up the phone and typed something into the computer. "One of the maids has a problem," she said. "That old white guy with the bleached hair." Smooshie wasn't someone who smiled much or bothered to explain, and she didn't call them gentlemen. "Room 886," she said.

I stood there.

Her eyebrows drew together and she locked her gaze on me. "So go up there."

On the eighth floor, the maid complaining downstairs had already returned to her cart where she stood, staring down at her cell phone. She clucked at me as I passed. I was irritated enough to wheel around. I was not proceeding any farther until she was well down the hall. In fact, I followed her. We glared at each other as the elevator doors pulled shut. Most likely a guest would have seen this hand-to-hand combat as nation against nation, but it was just two individuals caught in differently-shaded foul moods.

When I opened the door to Room 886, the strong scent of bath gel greeted me. A recent shower had left the room weighted with humidity. Mr. Smith was lying on the bed, motionless, his eyes closed peacefully. His ironed pristine khakis were pulled on and buckled. A starched blue shirt was neatly tucked in. The arms of an orange sweater were tied around his neck so that it fell about his collar as an insouciant bowtie. He was barefoot and his feet below the ironed khaki pants looked, well, I can think of no other word for it: happy. His feet were happy and naked. Unironed feet against the starchness of his clothes. The toes were long and visibly jointed and knuckly, as if they might have their own life as gainfully active equals to his hands.

Spread out on the bed like this, Mr. Smith seemed like a beachcomber contentedly drunk upon the sand. His wrists were handcuffed to the bar across the headboard. Next to him on the royally immense bed was space enough for another spread-eagled body. I glanced to see if the mattress and bedspread had been disturbed in any way. All was smooth beside him.

With that, just as my observations came to a close, Mr. Smith opened his eyes. He stared up at me with a smile. He was clearly waiting for me to say something, but I did not.

"Forty winks and I wake up to this," he said.

"Do you have keys?" I asked.

"Don't know," he said. "Do I?"

I felt around the night stand, then down on the carpet. "I think it's right here," he told me. His shackled hand twisted so that the finger could point downward. The key had fallen against the pillow. I undid his first wrist, but he did not move his arm from its overhead position. Because of how he watched me, somewhat amused, as if I were the one exposing myself to such humiliation, I couldn't make myself lean over his chest to undo the second wrist. I walked around to the other side of the huge bed and leaned across the emptiness of a phantom body.

He sat up and sighed contentedly. He didn't bother to rub his wrists. There were no red streaks or signs of wear on them.

"Your hotel is very dangerous. I'm lucky nothing bad happened," he said. "This could have been a lot worse, and then what? Thank you by the way for coming to the rescue. A lawsuit? Come here, let me show you."

He stood up to offer me his seat on the bed. I sat down. This was the first time I had sat on any of the beds. For moments longer than I must have been aware of, I dreamed of spreading myself upon it and falling asleep. When I glanced up, Mr. Smith was going through his wallet.

"I wonder what those black eyes of yours would look like..." He paused, although it would be misleading to say his voice hesitated. He was not the type of man to hesitate. He let the sentence fade out quite as a singer might turn down the dial on his notes. "I would call them luminescent."

By now I think he knew his important role as my English teacher. "Fluorescent?"

Each word pulled me closer.

From his wallet he removed a five and several singles and reached down to tuck them under my belt. He peered at my crotch. He pulled out another dollar bill and slid it between the buttons of my shirt. I'm afraid I must have disappointed him. For many months every pretty woman, every old beggar on the sidewalk, every dying widow had been an object of my desire. Yet here I was, no longer a man I could distinguish from any other. Like my name I was thousands of others, thousands upon thousands. In the end I was Tesfai, nothing at all, and it would take more than this to have the life breathed into me. The bills he tucked inside me would find a good home. I would hide them from my nephew and save them for the wife and children who were everything to me and nothing.

A Modified Cylinder

SHE ARRIVED AT THE HOUSE BY JITNEY. Cameron
had promised to cover transportation costs, but he made lots of
promises and she couldn't count on reimbursement. A regular taxi
this far out in the country would cost at least forty or fifty dollars
one way. Her apprentice salary was low, the same as all the others,
despite the discrepancy in merit, despite the fact that she had
virtually taken over for Cameron at the wax museum. The jitney
driver appeared to realize they were in the same boat. He was poor
as well but, like her, seemed to have ambition. They negotiated
for thirty dollars round trip. He turned his radio to a classical
music station for the duration of the ride, and when he left her at
her destination bowed and said softy, "Peace and blessings." She
couldn't place his accent.

Together the man and woman opened the door. Their names
were Jeremy and Patricia Hengley. They were longtime personal
friends of Cameron but he had sent her, Antoinette Oliver, an
apprentice, rather than go himself. She walked into their home.
Jeremy Hengley carried in the cooler where Annie kept the wax,
softened with animal fat, and then motioned her to a leather chair.
The inside of the house was grand. The living area opened up to a
cathedral ceiling and exposed beams. The furnishings, spare and
gleaming, reminded her of a Lutheran church.

After she sat, the man, Jeremy, asked if he could get her an iced tea
to beat back the summer heat. She looked to her hands, a reflex not

a reproach, and immediately he sputtered over himself in apology. She said, "No, something hot would be fine. Coffee or tea, if you have it, in a mug. I like to wrap my hands around something warm."

"Part of your warm-up routine," he weakly joked.

"Something like that," she laughed. But the room refused to lighten up.

The wife, Patricia, sat, her own hands twisted into repose, trying to be calm.

Jeremy said, "I'm sorry, I won't pretend. Cream? We're very nervous."

Patricia added, "This is probably your most unusual — oh, um, what do you call it? Assignment?"

"Our profession is unusual to begin with. Just black is fine, thank you."

The awkward silence stretched into something worse. She was glad when the man set the mug on a coaster and she had something to do. She picked it up and the warmth bled into her palms. She said, "Please, any questions you need to ask, go ahead. I'll answer."

"You're so young," Patricia said.

"I'm thirty."

"Exactly thirty?"

"Exactly."

"You look younger but you act older. Are you French?" Jeremy asked.

"What? No."

"Antoinette Oliver. That's French, isn't it?"

"I just go by Annie."

"You were an art major, I assume," his wife interrupted.

"Anatomy."

"Oh. That could be quite helpful, I suppose."

"Well it is." She was going for the proper tone of assent, but it came out wrong, as if she were sighing in frustration at them.

After another silence she added, "Are you sure there aren't more questions? Techniques, process?"

"We've been learning about those," the husband said. "And the other apprentices here the last two days, they've been filling us in. We understand you do something different from the rest of them."

Annie took a sip of coffee, then flexed her digital tendons against the mug. This didn't go unnoticed by Patricia and Jeremy. Her fingers were beginning to feel thickened from the heat so she replaced the mug on the coaster. She looked over at the couple. A nice couple. Good parents, clearly. Wealthy. It was not exactly a time to be modest, was it? Modesty was a good defense, but their predatory nervousness required offense. She was filled with unease and, unusual for her, a sense of impending failure. The sadness in the house was creeping in.

The wife took a deep breath, then plunged in with her real question. "Why isn't Cameron doing it himself?"

"It's quite natural to have the apprentices do all the set-up work," Annie told her.

"We understand that. We've had two days of exhaustive measurements. If I ever see another caliper!" The woman was ablaze with a self-reproachful annoyance.

"I'm here to make the final portrait," Annie said. "I guess that's where your hesitation lies — in having me do it instead of Cameron. Since I'm officially an apprentice, too."

"And apprentices don't do that, we've taken it to understand. Finish work, I guess you'd call it," the husband said, his light pun laced with acid.

"Right," Annie agreed. "Apprentices usually don't." It was getting hard to maintain that meditative calm she always strove for.

The man nodded toward her hands. "Cameron said he was sending his 'most gifted apprentice.' That's what he called you."

"We're flattered, of course," Patricia said.

"But he used that word, 'apprentice,' he made sure to use that word."

"Gifted, of course, but apprentice, too."

The man and woman hung their heads, clearly ashamed, yet driven to say it. "Cameron is ill," Annie told them.

"He didn't tell us that."

"I'm sorry, that's really all I can say."

The man said, "If I were to assume an illness based on what I've long assumed to be his lifestyle, would that be the illness we're talking about?"

"Jeremy," his wife corrected.

He shrugged. "As long as we're being painfully honest, I've always had to read between the lines with Cameron. Everything he says is an exaggeration, usually disguised as flattery of another person, yet anything but sincere praise due to its flagrant overstatement."

"Jeremy," his wife said.

"Well he's bitter that he's considered an artisan rather than the true artist he thinks he is."

"The money should have helped him get over that." Patricia chuckled tartly, as if she herself had been cheated out of wealth.

"Money he doesn't share, I bet." The man turned to Annie, but she gave him no reaction. She knew Cameron was rich. She knew he was insufferable about it. His claims that it was due to an artistic meritocracy rather than the attraction of a wax museum to low-brow tourists, exactly the kind of people Cameron would cruelly mock, simply revealed his own insecurity. So he ran a wax museum for his money, so what. Now that he was ill, he was starting to take his artistic bitterness out on others.

"Cameron didn't flatter you," the husband informed Annie. "He didn't do that damning with overstated praise bit. You're gifted, he allowed, but he also said 'apprentice,' he made sure to hammer that word home, and he made it clear you were almost at his level but not quite, no, not quite at all. That's not the usual Cameron approach. Which would be to say 'Oh she's fantastic beyond fantastic, she's superb, she does things with wax I could never dream of!' Which of course is a bunch of typical Cameron bombast meaning you offer not the slightest challenge to him."

"Yes, that sounds like Cameron," his wife agreed.

"So is he intimidated by you — by these 'gifts,' for instance — or just the opposite, too sick, too uncaring?"

"I am different," she said. "It's true. Whether you want to call it Art or not is up to you. I can do what I do. It's not unprecedented. Patience Wright was renowned for it." The man and woman stared at her blankly. "A famous wax artist, Patience Wright. She was a friend of Benjamin Franklin's."

"Obviously, the name Benjamin Franklin is familiar," the man said.

"Anyway, she worked the same way I do."

"Which is how? Cameron says you don't even have to look."

"Well, after I've looked initially, of course. Patience Wright worked with the wax between her legs, hidden and warmed by an apron. Once she started, she never looked at what her hands were doing."

"You keep mentioning Patience Wright."

"Because I've adopted the same approach."

"And this is something Cameron can't do?"

"Correct."

They said nothing. They waited for her to continue.

"So to answer your question... Well, perhaps there's no better time to say it out loud. It's important for you to know, I'm sure. I have a special talent. Beyond Cameron's? Because of your unique situation I'll answer truthfully: Yes."

Patricia Hengley sighed gratefully. "I just knew. I'm sorry. I'm just so thankful."

"So you just put the ball of wax under your apron and knead away," Jeremy Hengley said with an arch breeziness.

"I suppose."

"Like bread. What's in front of you hardly matters. It — he or she, that is — is just a thing. A loaf of bread. I take issue with that, you see. Our daughter's much more than a loaf of bread."

"No, no. Please understand. It's exactly the opposite." Now she was the one feeling nervous. She'd heard about the drowning some time ago, from Cameron in another context. When it came up again as *this,* this project, she was dumbfounded. It wasn't the bizarreness of the proposal — death masks had been the typical way to memorialize, and then later tintypes of the recently deceased child posed in their finest clothing — it was the fact that Cameron had chosen to send her. He knew her gifts didn't work that way. She needed the heat of breath, an ardent pulse tapping out the full portrait of its message. Cameron didn't require her talent to do what amounted to a lifeless mask.

"You don't look artistic," Jeremy Hengley commented. "I mean, not like those others who came here. You look more like someone in law school."

"He means it as a compliment," his wife said. "I went to law school, right, Jeremy?"

"Of course I do." He turned to accept his wife's hands in his own. After a cough that he tried to make sound real, he said, "It's just that we need to know. It's not like we'll have another chance at this. He coughed again so that he could turn away and hide his suddenly contorted face.

Patricia Hengley interrupted. "I just want you to know I'm so grateful."

At that moment a door upstairs opened and clicked carefully shut, and a child about six years old appeared on the stairway. She wore a sundress that showed off her beautiful arms and shoulders, glowing from the sun's caress, the *slightest* caress, for clearly Patricia and Jeremy were the kind of parents who were almost too careful, who would not let this lovely child out the door without sunscreen and a hat. In the girl's arm was an old stuffed animal, species unrecognizable in its eyeless floppiness. Around its neck was a crumpled ribbon, the same kind as in the child's long curls.

"Honey, we told you that—"

"Remember, we explained."

"I'm sure she loves little girls, but she needs to..."

"I want to come down now," the child said, not in a whiny manner but rather in a most pleasant way.

The precise bashful voice floated down like gauze. Seeing the lovely girl, Annie felt the pressure in her head begin to drift away. As the child drew closer, she began to feel it. Something extra lived within the child.

"I'm sorry," the woman apologized. "She's overeager. This is our daughter, Melanie." She looked at the girl, the tears starting.

"It's all right," Annie said. "It's fine. In fact, I think it's time. Is Melanie allowed to visit?"

"Oh yes. They're best friends. Right, darling?"

Melanie smiled.

"I'm ready then. Could you take me to your sister, Melanie?"

The little girl held out her hand. Annie reached, needing to feel the serene mildness of the child's skin, but Patricia Hengley had already interceded and grasped hold of Melanie. They climbed the stairs and moved in a silent march down the long hall. The house was new, built within the last six or seven years, a Tudor hybrid set adrift in a clear-cut swath of deep green countryside, the immature, toothpick-like trees offering scant privacy from the other houses. From a majestic window in the hall she saw the pool in the backyard, its peaceful blue sheet of water anything but the sky's real color. Around the perimeter of the pool an imposing fence with a locked gate had been erected.

Melanie came to the door and did not hesitate to open it. She gaily skipped into the bedroom even as her parents drew back. Annie followed her inside. There lay the child. The respirator drew back a sucking sound after each breath it forced into the child's lungs. A false diaphragm moved up and down in the pump.

Already the switch to turn off the machine beckoned Annie. How had they resisted for six years?

"Our older daughter's name is Cynthia," the woman said from the doorway. The man's arm came round his wife's shoulder. Annie felt their fear and embarrassment, and now their grief. Once her work was done, the respirator would finally be turned off, Cynthia's body would be buried and this wax model would take its place. Or so Cameron had told her. How they had chosen to live this way for so long was not for Annie to fathom. She mustn't think about it. She simply had a job to do.

She removed the work apron from her handbag and tied it on. The apron was lined with a woolen quilting to keep the wax warm. The man and woman watched her. "Benjamin Franklin's friend," the man whisper-scoffed. His wife pulled him back into the shadows of the hallway.

Annie sat down next to Cynthia. She tried to ignore the motor thrusts of breathing. The girl was much larger than she had expected. The same age as Melanie when the drowning occurred, she had been declared brain dead at age six, but her physical body had enlarged into age twelve. Though her chest appeared flat to the eye, when Annie put her hand to the girl's heart, she could feel the breasts beginning to rise. Puberty was not far off.

Her hand remained over Cynthia's heart. The organ — for it was an organ now, not a heart — beat thick, mechanized thrubs against her hand. It was an instrument being played by a machine.

She could not even call it a drum, a distant drum. It carried no far-off message. It carried no personal rhythm.

She stroked Cynthia's arm, then picked up the hand and curled the fingers. The hand was nothing. The fingers were nothing. The skin was nothing. Annie's own hands, which should have been crackling with sparks, fighting to get to the wax, were instead growing numb. She was touching living death, and the feel of it was bituminous, hard and soft, and in the end nothing more than a fossil fuel. Why had Cameron sent her here? Why not someone else? What her hands possessed, an ability to bring the wax alive, would not work here. She had lifelessness to work with, and lifelessness to imitate. The poorest wax artist could have accomplish that much; in fact, the poorest wax artist would have been most suitable for the job. Had he wanted her to fail? Did Cameron care so little about Patricia and Jeremy that her failure was more satisfying than helping longtime friends close their circle of grief? Annie knew it was so.

Melanie bounced over to her older sister. She held her floppy animal above Cynthia's face and jumped him from invisible cloud to invisible cloud. She chattered. She had known her sister in no other capacity than this, Annie realized. The glow of Melanie's little girl beauty startled Annie anew, and her hands began to come alive. She asked Melanie to sit there beside her. "May I?" Annie asked, reaching out to the stuffed animal. Melanie let Annie wrap her arms round her, and together they showed the animal to Cynthia. Slowly, Annie encouraged the animal to drop away, and their pairs of hands, fingers intertwined, rested on Cynthia's chest, nothing else but their hands and Cynthia's heart, becoming more a heart now, and above the heart her left breast, poised to grow. They sat, and touched, until Annie's nerve endings, charged and thickened as telephone cables, could no longer stand it.

After a time Annie got up from the bed. She opened up the cooler and retrieved the large ball of wax. She secreted the wax under her apron where, warmed and sparked to life, she began to knead it. She sat back on the bed. Melanie watched her with a quiet excitement. Annie flipped the apron back and quickly unearthed the beginnings of Cynthia's face on the wax. Then she stood up, turning her back to her subject. Here was where Cameron tried so hard not to be awestruck. Whatever it was she possessed — it was unimportant to her to name it — it allowed her to work blindly, the wax held under the warming apron. She walked to the window and looked out while her hands molded on their own. Her mind could wander freely to other things. She saw across the road to the other houses, a mix-n-match of styles, for the owners had selected their own designs. The Georgian one, particularly, looked out of place with its cold white columns plunging into a treeless rug of lawn. A driveway to another house was being reblackened. A bucket of tar stood at either boundary and acted as stakes for the orange tape stretched across the sticky shine. The woods were still visible in the distance: mossy-colored and dense, abandoned for the time being, a defiant entanglement. Soon, like wax, the trees would be pounded down and a subdivision raised in its place. Something artificial, but satisfying.

Cameron had given his apprentices three rules to live by:

Skull size doesn't matter, etcetera on downward

Bad statues and rigor mortis look the same

Human beings are modified cylinders

To Annie, however, whose ability bypassed all the rules, there was only one thing to remember, a single, sad observation: for those created in wax, it was the same story. Always the same story. Always and forever the same story.

Behind her she heard the sucking of the respirator. In and out, then catching. The deep, almost watery breaths overpowered the machine's pumping. They belonged to someone else, she realized, not to Cynthia but to Cynthia's father. Jeremy. She knew without looking he was standing at the door. The hard, controlled breaths were a man's battle against weeping. The sounds quickly retreated as she began to turn around, and she heard footsteps, one pair running, one pair chasing.

She went back to looking outside. She wished Cynthia had had a big tree by her window, a squirrel at least to tap on the glass these past six years. In their front yard she saw the For Sale sign. She had barely registered it as she arrived. Well, good luck to them. Prospective buyers would surely ask about the locked and gated pool. They would not like such a forbidding structure enclosing their summer fun and would ask why it was there.

Her hands stopped. She was finished. She turned around and Melanie was still there, still talking in happy whispers to Cynthia and the floppy animal. Melanie looked up and saw the molded head emerge from under the apron. The child jumped up, delighted. "It's Cynthia!" she cried. "Bye, Cynthia," she waved as Annie laid the head into the cooler and snapped the lid.

As she and Melanie left the bedroom, neither Patricia nor Jeremy Hengley was anywhere to be seen. They were hiding somewhere, comforting each other, waiting for her to go. She understood that she would not be seen out. She proceeded down the stairs, opened the front door, and went outside. White wicker furniture was arranged on the porch, but she chose to sit on the steps, and Melanie sat next to her. The cement was warm, the stippled surface like the pricks of her own nerve endings, now dying down. She stuffed the apron in her handbag. Her palms as usual were experiencing a type of freezer burn on their surface. Beside her Melanie glowed, almost surreal in her beauty. Annie was compelled to put her arm around her, to touch the delicate muscles of the little girl's arm, to loop her thumb and finger around the wrist. How wonderful the small limbs felt, how vividly the extra life thrummed against her.

Down the street she saw the jitney puttering around a bend. It began a slow, awkward turn into the long drive. The glow from the little girl spurted large and forceful — holding Melanie close to her as she was, Annie felt the neck's pulse, a sudden, almost sexual swell of blood — and then the glow pulsated downward, fading, and then soothed into nothing. When she looked at Melanie again, she saw a pretty little girl — pretty, but not alarming in her beauty, not unearthly. A little girl. Just that.

The jitney driver had stopped the car and positioned himself beside the passenger door like a chauffeur. He was looking at the house. His gaze had been drawn upward, toward Cynthia's window. Annie had to control herself not to join him in looking there.

"Good-bye," she said to Melanie, giving her a kiss.

Melanie patted the cooler as she stood up. "Can I see Cynthia one more time before you go? I mean, may I? Please?"

"You'll see her again," Annie told the little girl. "I promise. In just a few weeks you'll have your sister back home."

After Lunch

ESKRICH OF LATE HAD grown suspicious. His legs always let him know. In the expensive restaurants where he was a daily customer, he had begun to notice alert ears cocked his way. The waiters lingered, combing non-existent crumbs from the tablecloth. Eskrich was forced to pause the conversation, which furthered the effect that it was something not to be overhead. It *was* something not to be overheard. Now, Eskrich was sure, everyone was overhearing it.

Thus, for good reason, Eskrich began eating at a budget cafeteria where the clientele was mostly aged. Almost immediately he felt calmer. His legs paused their painful twitching. The cafeteria offered incapacitated ears and a sloth-like pace. He began to look forward to the ritual of pushing his plastic tray along the brushed steel bars and watching the food roll by like fake scenery. The elderly women poked along authoritatively, steering their guests away from the lead-off treats with the assurance that better desserts lay ahead. The ones who weren't widowed ushered husbands who had rewarded their wives' loyalty by becoming entirely useless. The women, thinking ahead, laid a quarter tip on the tray for the worker who carried their husband's meal.

The corner table Eskrich now thought of as his own was a four-seater. Though it was bad form among the careful seniors to grab a spot larger than needed, he nevertheless folded his suit jacket over one of the chairs, claiming the bigger table as his own, before going through the line.

Eskrich had tried out the cafeteria with a couple of zoning commissioners, one from the town of Mt. Levington and the other from Mapleport. Both of them had liked it. The comfort food had made their conversation about rezoning some farmland for a big-box retailer feel friendly and natural, but they were from the country, these fellows, and this kind of place suited them.

Today Eskrich had brought Sunderson here. Sunderson was a man who liked to talk. When he drank, he talked more and he talked more loudly. In fact, it was Sunderson with his big body and big laugh and big stories who had first made Eskrich begin to squirm so at his old upscale restaurants. Every time one of these restaurants got popular the tables started edging closer and closer together. Squeezing in more people until people got squeezed out. He should have written a letter. Has your eating establishment ever heard of an intimate atmosphere or the need for a private conversation? Move the kitchen back inside, we get it already, and make room for the paying customers. Of course at his table nothing exactly illegal had ever been said — Eskrich if anything was a master of the *nothing exactly* — but to discerning ears who had also mastered the same game, fill-in-the-blank phrasings were enough to give yourself away. Eskrich began to see the boys with their peppermills, always a dreaded sight anyway, though a new set of terrors. He heard them clanging their spiced blackjacks against his prison bars. Finally one noon his legs, twitching and painful, could stand it no longer. He threw down his linen napkin and ran from the wine-sipping eavesdroppers. Outside he dialed Sunderson on his cell phone and told him he had sprained his ankle and was at the hospital. He hadn't seen Sunderson since, until today.

Sunderson was ahead of him in the cafeteria line. By now Eskrich had learned a few of the tricks the old ladies knew, the most basic being don't get smitten by the Jello parfaits and the tapioca and the pretty mandarin oranges. He found himself wanting to correct Sunderson when he fell for these majorettes leading off the parade of dishes. Sunderson chose not only the tricolor Jello cubes, but the pink-tinted pudding as well. Then he went for the pineapple cottage cheese. The grape that topped it looked like a bruised thumb sticking through. Eskrich wondered if Sunderson as well mistook the grape for a thumb, for at that moment Sunderson laughed out loud. The server laughed with him, sure of his good nature. "Jesus," Sunderson said to the server, "I haven't seen a hairnet since, Christ, ten years?" Eskrich cringed at the profanity. This was a cafeteria. It was one step below a church. Many of the people held hands and prayed before they ate.

"I got long hair," the server said. "Been growing it all my life."

"Can you still buy those hair things or do you have to go to an antique store?" The server began to answer in earnest but Sunderson interrupted. "Sweetheart, what is this on top of the pudding, a butter pat?"

"That's whipped cream."

"It looks like a butter pat. Put some real whipped cream on this, would you, sweetheart?"

Sunderson went through the line like this, adjusting his portions, more green beans, more stewed cabbage, a bigger slice of prime rib, the biggest chicken breast you got there, more mashed potatoes and more gravy, and he made them go back into the kitchen to cut a bigger piece of Dutch apple pie. Eskrich watched amazed that the servers complied. Not only did they comply, they complied happily, even hungrily, as if convinced Sunderson were some kind of movie star. Sunderson was so out of place that he had to have been. He was a middle-aged white man who wore a diamond pimp necklace plopped over his collar and tie, and he laughed at everything in such a way as to say, I own this and it amuses me. Something was up and the servers knew it. They were electrified by this fantasy figure playing a drumbeat on his tray. This guy was a producer and he was watching them, probably for one of those reality TV shows. They scrambled to please him, increasing portions, arranging their spoken pleasantries and bright smiles, all of them working hard to have a successful audition.

Even in this place it began — Eskrich's nerves, the twitching in his legs. Sunderson did that to him.

At the end of the parade of dishes came the drinks. Sunderson asked an elderly woman in line to grab him that bottle of beer staked into the ice. Then he asked her to grab him one of those miniature bottles of red wine while she was at it. "And I'll be paying for this lovely young lady beside me," Sunderson told the cashier, which meant that Eskrich paid for it.

Sunderson had piled on three times as much food as Eskrich. At their table Eskrich forced himself to eat slowly, with long sips of coffee. He didn't want to have to sit there with empty hands. One of the servers came by with a refill, a first, since there was a self-serve beverage bar in the center of the dining room. Sunderson ate with the sloppy abandon of someone used to being in charge. Eskrich recognized it from interviews he had sat in on. He saw the same kind of power gluttony in the football and basketball coaches he ate with as an alumni booster, in the differences between how a heavily recruited athlete ate versus a merely hopeful one out to please. Sunderson was the director of downtown development. It sounded like an impressive job, but it didn't make him rich by any means. Sunderson's wife was a partner in a local law firm and for most people that explained the house in a gated community, and the boat and the second homes in Florida and Park City, Utah, but Sunderson's good life clichés depended on the donations developers like Eskrich threw his way.

Yet another server came by with more coffee and asked if everything was okay. Sunderson's mouth was stuffed full, but that didn't stop him from opening it. It's *something something* great, sweetheart, he told her. *Something something. Something.* Both Eskrich and the server stupidly watched Sunderson's mouth for enunciation clues. It wouldn't matter if they could understand him. Sunderson's conversation never made any sense. He threw out non-sequiturs like football plays. Eskrich's legs were hurting now — the cardinal sign that Sunderson was nearby.

To Sunderson's chomping mouth the server said, "I just want to tell you that that sweet old lady was so tickled you paid for her wine and lunch. She lost her husband a few months ago, it just meant the world..." Eskrich could see that Sunderson, his big rapacious Adam's apple flying up and down in his throat, was paying not one whit of attention. Eskrich quickly directed the server to one of the two-seater tables where another elderly woman sat alone, raising her hand like a second grader for more coffee. She had raised her hand the first time the server had come by with coffee warm-ups. A cane hung over the empty chair. Of all people, they should be refilling her cup, and the cups of people like her, not his and Sunderson's.

As she left, the server placed the cafeteria's business card on the table along with her handprinted name: *Sallie.*

Eskrich had seen the hand-raising old woman before. She had been brave and impolite enough to claim a four-seater and she wasn't even wearing a suit and tie and pimp necklace. He admired that. He was sure she had been sitting with her husband the last time he'd seen her, next to him rather than across from him. He had thought the cane belonged to him. Now she was alone, eating from her tray, not bothering to set out the dishes.

Eskrich wondered where the husband was. He couldn't have died so quickly. It was just a couple of days ago.

Sunderson was now picking the yellow cubes out of his tri-color Jello and slurping them down like oysters. Left were the red and green cubes. The wobbling colors reminded Eskrich of the eye exams he had taken as a child. The eye doctor's assistant strapped something around his eyes and he had to stare at a diamond of four lights. She asked him how many of the four spots were red. Three, he'd say. And how many are green? Two and a half, he'd say. That adds up to five and a half, not four, the assistant would say. The assistant was always irritated. He had weak eyes and it seemed he was back in that chair every month giving the wrong answers. But those wrong answers were the right answers, dammit. There *were* two and half green lights. Was he supposed to lie about it?

The server was back at their table, asking Sunderson if he'd like his pie heated up and a nice scoop of French vanilla ice cream placed on top of it.

Eskrich excused himself and inside the restroom dialed his cell phone.

"Have the two boys had their eyes checked?" he asked his wife.

"What are you talking about?"

"Don't you think they should be given eye exams? What if they've got my bad eyes?"

His wife said, "One is writing college applications. The other is fourteen. If they can't see, they can use their words to tell us."

"Their eyes should be dilated and their retinas checked."

"I can always tell when you're having one of those lunches," his wife told him.

"But have you ever taken them to be tested?"

"Have you?"

"Well no."

"I'm busy right now," his wife said and hung up.

Eskrich bumped the hand-raising old woman's table on the way back, not that hard, it was just an accident, but her coffee swished over and her cane fell off the chair. Since she used her tray as the coffee saucer, her chicken-n-noodles plate was now swamped in a black puddle. He didn't know what to do. He knew what Sunderson would do. Sunderson would do nothing because he wouldn't have noticed. The old woman hadn't started to get bony. Maybe she wasn't as old as the others. What happened to your husband? he wanted to ask her. He looked around for one of the servers. Knocking against the table had jolted his legs. He barged in at the cash register and told the cashier he needed help cleaning a spill. The path back to his table skirted the same old woman not as bony as the others and now her husband *was* there. He was shimmering in his seat, not looking very pleased. Not looking very human either. Eskrich returned to the restroom and called his wife.

"I just saw a dead person," he said. "In the flesh."

"You're having lunch with Sunderson, aren't you?" his wife said.

"My legs are hurting."

"Drink more water," she said.

"No, I mean they're hurting again."

"I didn't know they were hurting before."

"Who's our doctor?" he asked.

"Why do you want to know?"

"I know we have one."

"Did you drink water with your lunch?"

"Could you call the doctor for me?"

"You call her."

"*Her?*"

"Call her and tell her your legs hurt."

"Why is Albert barking?"

"That's Steinway. Can't you tell their barks apart?"

One of his wife's most annoying qualities had resurfaced, this vibe she carried around for all the world to experience: *I love animals and do not think you can love them as much as I do.*

"What's the doctor's number?" he asked her. "I don't even know her name. You call, please. I'll never ask you to do anything else."

"Hold on." She hung up.

Eskrich slumped on the toilet while he waited and through the crack watched an old man in red pants stand in front of the urinal. He was still standing there when his wife called back five minutes later.

"She said exactly what I thought she'd say. She can't see you today."

"Why not?"

"She said go the emergency room if they keep hurting."

"It's not an emergency."

"Then don't bother me with it."

"Why can't she see me today?"

"She can see you in a week."

"I want to see her today."

"Why didn't you tell me last week they were hurting. Then she could have seen you today."

"That's not helpful," Eskrich said.

"She said Advil might work." Then his wife hung up.

The layout of the dining room, though he had grown used to it, was a game they played to trick the old people, which was not nice. That, too, was getting on Eskrich's nerves. It was sectioned off by low walls that mimicked separate dining rooms. Everything was dark. It was embarrassing to be lost, even in this place. He started going corner to corner within the sectioned areas until he found him. Sunderson's dishes were piled high like a sight gag. He was starting in on the Dutch apple pie, heated up, with the ice cream melting down the sides.

"Hey man, something's come up," Eskrich said. He tried for a long-suffering shrug. "I have to take off early."

Sunderson's stuffed mouth moved energetically. The sounds came pretty close to arf arf arf.

"I gottta go," Eskrich said. "I just wanted to reconnect."

Sunderson held up a finger, swallowed. "Let's do it again."

"This a good place for you to meet then?

"Great *something something,*" Sunderson said, forking in the pie.

Eskrich spent the rest of the afternoon in the emergency room, outranked by real emergencies. Just as his moment approached, a boy came in bleeding all over the place. Nurses ran out with towels. There was a lot of blood. When his name was finally called, Eskrich asked the nurse about the boy.

"Is he going to be okay?"

"I can't talk about other patients."

"Yeah, I know," Eskrich said, "but can you find a way to talk about him anyway?"

"All I can tell you is that scalp wounds bleed a lot." The nurse looked down at the info sheet. "You write here that both your parents are deceased from no cause of death."

"That's right."

"They didn't die of anything?"

"No. My dad had all these moles on his chest. Every week he'd get more. He looked like a hairy chocolate chip cookie."

"Do you think that contributed to his death?" the nurse asked.

"People always thought so. I don't know. From the neck up he looked normal."

"How old was he when he died?"

"Somewhere in his fifties. Is that little boy okay?"

"Were the moles malignant?" the nurse asked.

"No. He had a heart attack."

"A heart attack," the nurse repeated. "So he did have a cause of death."

"Yeah I guess when you put it like that."

"And your mother. Did she have heart attack that might have caused her death?"

"She's still alive actually. I just think of her as dead."

"Does she have any chronic illnesses, a heart condition, cancer?"

"No."

"Diabetes, high blood pressure?"

"No. Do scalp wounds really bleed that much?"

"They can."

"Did he get shot?"

"He's eight years old," the nurse said.

"Eight year olds can get shot."

"He didn't get shot. Have you been like this for long?"

"Like what?"

"Irrational."

"I'm not irrational," Eskrich told her.

"So you don't know when it started," the nurse concluded.

"No, I guess I don't."

"All right," she said, "we're going to take a CAT scan."

Afterwards, Eskrich had time for a nap. When the intern strolled in, Eskrich's first thought was white guy, not a Jew. Not an Indian. An American like himself.

"Mr. Eskrich," the intern said.

"That's me."

"How are you feeling?"

"Good!"

"Really..."

Eskrich's high hopes for bonding were dashed. "Shouldn't I be feeling okay?"

"I can't tell you how you should be feeling, but you've got blood clots in your legs."

"Plural?"

"Yes."

"Big ones?"

"Small ones."

"Little tiny ones?"

"Pretty small, yes."

"So that's good then."

"Nooo," the intern said. "We can give you medication for the pain, if you'd like."

"All right."

"I thought you were feeling fine," the intern said. "Now you want pain medication. We need to know if you're in pain."

"I'm just trying to agree with you. Helping us both to get out of here quicker, right?"

"Let me see if the oncologist is here yet." The intern left the room and Eskrich took out his cell phone and redialed his wife.

"It's me. I'm at the hospital."

"That was sudden. What did Sunderson do to you?"

"Have you made the eye appointments for the boys yet?" he asked.

"Not yet."

"Just promise me you will."

"Why are you at the hospital?"

"Because I couldn't get a regular appointment with her — that doctor of ours. When did we get a *her* doctor?"

"Don't use the cell phone in here," the intern said as he returned.

"Things are happening quickly. Gotta go," he said into phone.

"Was that your wife?" the intern asked.

"Yes."

"Did you tell her to come to the hospital?"

"No reason to."

"Our nurses will call. The oncologist isn't here yet."

"I know what the word 'oncologist' means."

"Besides the blood clots, you've got several spots on your liver."

"Is that bad?"

"We never like to see spots of that nature. We never like to see them on the liver."

"So *of that nature* means it's bad."

"I don't want to speak without a specialist here."

"Well..." Eskrich stopped. "Could you find a way to talk about it anyway?"

"Hold on," the intern said and left.

"I used to be a swimmer," Eskrich called after him. He used to carry a tray with six glasses of milk on it and lots of food. His wife, he realized had the same shape as Sunderson, both of them unusually tall with narrow shoulders sloping to a wide spread in the stomach and hips. He imagined Sunderson's body with his wife's face on it, and then his wife's body with Sunderson's face on it. If there was one thing he really disliked about his wife, it was that her for-all-the-world-to-see vibe that *I love animals more than you do* (which was true) included the specific verdict that *I love Albert and Steinway more than you do* (which was not true).

The intern returned with an older man. He was dark with a salt-n-pepper beard. Thank God, a Jew, or maybe an Indian, hard to tell; either way he was saved. This was too much for an all-American boy to handle. Eskrich breathed a huge sigh of relief. The oncologist held out his hand and introduced himself. He carried himself with gravity. The wiry beard trickled up to his cheekbones. Finally, a real doctor. "Hello, doctor," Eskrich said. Just saying the word 'doctor' made him feel better. "I see you've got experience..." *something something.* Now he was Sunderson spouting nonsense. He just wanted to let this guy know the confidence he had in him, that he thought he was an expert M.D., just that he was on his side one hundred percent.

The doctor asked Eskrich to lie down. He told Eskrich everything he was doing. "I'm palpating your liver." Eskrich jerked. Then the hands were around his throat. "My hands are feeling your lymph nodes." Eskrich tried to escape the hands. He pulled away and came face to face with a football recruit jumping up from the luncheon table at Morton's and pumping his fist. He smelled the damp inside of his son's new used car. His other son looked up from the couch when he walked in, neither pleased nor annoyed to see his father, and didn't bother to take his feet off the coffee table. "How does that feel?" the doctor asked.

"There's a small white cloud floating above me," Eskrich said. "Am I still here?" There was actually a small white cloud. Though brief and quick, it was real. But probably he should not have mentioned it.

Now the doctor was pushing at him more and it hurt. "Tell me it's okay," Eskrich said. He steeled his face and the tightened muscles forced out tears. He couldn't stop the tears. The doctor had fallen silent. "Tell me!" The doctor looked away when Eskrich cried out, and Eskrich saw it clearly. The doctor was another person who didn't care whether he lived or died. Eskrich had succeeded in only one thing: he was boring the doctor to death.

If A Then B Then C

1.

Three years ago I was making a living as a realtor. The market was on fire. Even a newcomer like me could move houses. All I had to do was pull up to the curb in my car, pose in the yard by the For Sale sign and await my clients. Other potential buyers would usually be leaving as my home-hunters arrived. I simply waited for the bidding war to begin. It got so easy for those few months that I stopped dressing for success in high heels and a suit. One day towards the end I stood on the sidewalk in jogging pants and a T-shirt. More unsavory, my T-shirt was still wet with perspiration (I had decided to jog the mile to the showing). I was pinching it away from my throat, shaking it out to dry, when Charlotte rode up on her bicycle, followed by another woman and then a man. I took pity on Charlotte. I helped her through the closing, cutting down on my commission because this was her first house, it was shaving her dry, she'd gotten a loan she really shouldn't have qualified for. She was very pretty, very royalty even on a bicycle with a handbell. Then there was the matter of Charlotte's ex who wasn't quite an ex. After the fight he put up over dowager's rights, I'm sure I ended up losing money.

2.

I was out of the real estate business. I had left the game right before the fall with what appeared to be foresight on my part. In

actuality it was my short attention span. Another failed relationship plummeted me like the market. When I looked up, I was
managing a fitness chain. Now I was encouraged to dress in sweats.
I didn't. I was a very tall woman. I looked like a basketball coach.
One Saturday during a membership drive Bea Suffolk called me at
the club. How she knew where I was working I didn't know, but Bea
Suffolk was a digger. She had been the agent for the owners who
had sold their house to Charlotte. I said — the words a complete
shock to me — "This is about Charlotte, isn't it? She's dead."

"I wish," Bea said.

I was five minutes early for the Sunday lunch I had agreed to.
Bea was already there, fingering the stem of a wine glass. She was
always early, always prepared. She was a digger.

I was shocked when I saw her.

Bea believed realtors should have a signature style. They had a
specific territory; why not a specific style? Her signature was suits
that were almost too tight. She was single, a career woman, and
stayed looking much younger than her age by utilizing various
self-improvement programs during those ample hours stolen
from mothers and married women. The suit jackets she wore
were usually fastened by a single oversized brocaded button. They
gripped her waist before flaring out. They ended short, never
covering her rear end. She was always pushing her single button,
then tugging on the jacket's truffled hem.

In the three years since I'd last seen her, she had aged an
additional fifteen.

"You can say it," she said after I greeted her and sat down.

"Say what?"

She almost smiled, sipped on her wine. Before my glass arrived,
I heard about her South American parasite, leishmaniasis, her
failing health, her failure. Her failure, she shrugged. Failure. She
had not bothered to color her hair; the too brassy hue (also a

signature) had faded to dullness and was rooted in a wide furrow of white.

Now for her confession. I grabbed the wine from the waiter's tray and took a healthy swallow. She had been Charlotte's sugar mommy. Charlotte had betrayed her. Charlotte was out there somewhere.

She could see from my face I hadn't known.

"I thought you might have guessed," she said.

"No."

"Too busy softening up the almost ex-husband in that house mess."

"Too busy losing my commission."

"I'm sixty-eight years old," Bea told me. "And I'm pretty sure I'm dying."

When I didn't respond, Bea snapped her fingernail hard against my wine glass.

"Hey. Do you understand what I'm telling you?"

"I had no idea you were gay," I said.

3.

Here's what I think about Charlotte and it's not much because I didn't know her very well. Charlotte always struck me as misplaced in time. She got her way yes because she was pretty, but also because she appealed to an atavistic chivalry that charged through even the blood of females. And so I for one surrendered my commission. Barely knowing her, I spent two evenings drinking with her legal husband who kept wondering out loud about dykes and asking me to explain it to him in detail. I did. He signed. Another thing about being misplaced in time: Charlotte sauntered as if she were an empress, shedding layers of clothes. They dropped to the palace floor or to the humble earth. Of course others would pick them up. Who wouldn't rescue something clean from the mud?

4.

Bea told me this story about them. It was hard to believe. She was in love. Charlotte said she was in love. However, Charlotte had never bothered to learn the name of Bea's cat or the name of her schnauzer or the name of her labradoodle. In fact, Bea said, she hadn't even learned her name. Whose name? I asked. My name, Bea said. What? My name, Bea said. My name. Beatrice. Bea. My name.

5.

I drove to the house that three years earlier I had sold to Charlotte. I was surprised not to see a For Sale sign in its yard. I went up to the porch, peeked as best I could through the edges of the bay window. I followed the windows around the house. Edge by edge a picture of the downstairs accordioned together. The house was empty of people, as was typical during a work day, but it also keened its emptiness. There was furniture, unsheeted, arranged for conversation, but the pieces gaped vacantly at each other like lost souls.

Next door a woman sat on her front porch. She was old, too heavy, white hair afright. A cane leaned against the porch railing. Atop the railing lay a cordless phone. I asked her who lived here. She didn't answer. Does anyone live here? Foreclosure? I suggested. I mentioned Charlotte's name. Her mouth zipped right up.

6.

The fitness center I was managing offered something different from the other run-of-the mill treadmill factories: horseback riding. We had a stable at another location out in the countryside.

It was a disaster waiting to happen, this stable, especially now that the outerbelt was constructing new exits. More people meant more danger. The liability insurance, the future pending lawsuits, just the horses themselves and their hay. I knew I'd have to leave soon. I woke up one Tuesday and turned thirty seven and had to endure a surprise birthday party by my co-workers, held in the barn. I left early, my excuse the family-n-friends soirée awaiting me. I went alone to a pub many of my neighbors frequented. I could relax. My neighbors waved but they didn't know me well enough to wish me happy birthday.

7.

I wasn't the digger that Bea was, so she called me on the phone and delivered the information. I found Charlotte in front a Catholic elementary school. Children in plaid uniforms getting on buses. Children in plaid uniforms getting into soccermom vans. Charlotte didn't look any different. She was wearing a tight skirt patterned in swirling seahorses and talking to a teacher. She turned to leave with a big smile, still finishing her sentence. She walked her slightly duckwalk empress walk to the car. The two girls she was holding onto pulled up like stubborn cattle. Charlotte dropped their hands easily, shedding them from herself as if from a mink stole, and carried on alone, not looking back. The girls scampered after her and jumped into the backseat. She bent over and leaned in to check their seatbelts. When she stood up I was right beside her. She seemed very happy to see me again, and she responded instantly to the name Bea Suffolk. The girls were in their seatbelts; the key was in the ignition ready to be turned. I spoke quickly.

"Bea is dying and would like to see you."

"Okay," Charlotte agreed.

"Do you want to do it now?"

"Okay," Charlotte said.

I sat outside with the two girls while Charlotte went in alone. The girls were around seven or eight; they weren't twins but it was difficult to tell which one was older. I'd gone in first to let Bea know. Bea came out of the kitchen and settled into the bed she had moved downstairs. I plumped the pillows behind her head. Her hair had been newly colored. She looked good though appropriately withered.

I told the girls I liked their school outfits and they said "thank you very much" with a disarming sweetness. The wind had arrived in gusts. We watched a street sign begin to lurch. The clouds in the sky picked up speed. My mind left the cute girls. I thought about friends I'd lost touch with, friends I'd fought with, friends I saw in store aisles and made idle promises to. I thought about the two people I'd loved so deeply. I placed them each on a separate cloud. The wind took them quickly.

"Sometimes clouds look like things or people or animals," I said.

"I know," one of the girls said.

"I agree," piped up the other.

"My cloud looks like a magic carpet. What does your cloud look like?"

"My cloud looks like piano lessons," the one girl said.

"I agree," the other piped up.

"You must be the younger sister," I said to the agreeing girl.

Both girls giggled and snugged their shoulders into their neck.

Charlotte opened the front door and stepped out with a broad cleansing sigh. "That is so sad," she said. "That is so so sad."

"Are you sad, Charlotte Mommy?" the very adorable agreeing girl asked.

"Yes I am. I am so so sad."

The girls and I waited for Charlotte to go on. We stayed quiet. We looked up with expectant faces. We waited for it to be revealed. Charlotte turned to me. I knew right then, the look on her face, she didn't know my name. She asked if I could lead her back to the thru-way, she'd lost her bearings following me. So many streets. So many turns. She didn't know where in the world she was.

Vantage Point

THANKSGIVING DAY. The changeable Ohio weather has changed again. From the top of the hill Don Capachi can spot golfers in shirt sleeves. It's a pretty sight, the golf course, the mowed countryside that stretches around these little holes with flags sticking out of them. That's all the game used to be to him, but through the years he's watched from his secluded hill and learned more about it.

He has nowhere to go on Thanksgiving. He won't go to a restaurant or hotel and eat alone. He won't go to the free dinner at the convention center and take his place as an eighty-something sad sack. For the past ten Thanksgivings he's come here, and if the weather is warm enough, like today, he'll spread out a picnic blanket and watch the golfers squeeze in a game before football and turkey. Otherwise, he'll turn on the motor, adjust the heat, and eat in his car.

But today — what a warm beautiful day today is. He pops the trunk of his Buick, works the heavy bag of charcoal over the lip until the weight topples it to the ground. He drags it over to a bare spot, sets up a lawn chair, then looks up and freezes. He hears a noise. It's not a squirrel. Not the doe and her fawn he saw driving in. Not an animal at all. Someone else is here. That's never happened before, not on this day. He stops what he's doing.

A woman stands at one of the headstones, staring down. Her head bobs as she carries out both sides of the conversation. Don

Capachi backs up to a respectful distance. He waits, watches, bows solemnly to the woman when she finally leaves. Watches her go down the hill, her shoes crunching the leaves, to the car he had somehow failed to notice as he drove in (probably because his attention was on that lovely fawn, the smallest one he'd ever seen, as small as a beagle). When her car is out of sight, he walks over to where she stood, finds the flowers that mark the grave. He reads the stone. A set of parents, dead on the same day. Poor girl. No wonder she had a lot to say.

In summer the trees partially obstruct his view of the golf course. Not today. Don Capachi sets up the grill, gets the charcoal going. He plants the lawn chair several steps away. He won't need the charcoal's heat today. He carefully places two wieners on the grill.

Across the road a kind of crazy whooping noise spins the air. Striding to the 16th green are two happy men with their shirts off. It's warm but not that warm. They're young men, still able to maintain their shape even with a layer of beer fat. They look up and sniff the wiener-grilled air and laugh.

Don Capachi wonders suddenly where Worm is buried. Here in Ohio, or somewhere else?

They were about the same size, he and Worm, but Don Capachi had shrunk down to meet him. Was a time he was a lot bigger, a lot stronger. A lot younger, too. Goes without saying.

Worm was so young, so small. So stupid, too. Really, he was. In the end, he was so very stupid. Every day the sign in big red letters said it again: DO NOT LUBRICATE GEARS WHILE MACHINE IS RUNNING!

Why couldn't he just read the sign and obey it? Why did he have to be so stupid?

Don Capachi pours his favorite drink into a crystal tumbler and inhales the bouquet. Scotch, neat. Expensive scotch. He's got a cupboardful of the stuff, blended and single; he collects and sorts them like different grades of copper. Blended's for everyday. Single's for special occasions. He'll often decree a day a special occasion just to get a dip of it: a blue moon, a Friday the 13th, a ride home without any red lights, a day with no telephone solicitations. Those graced evenings bring him single malts. But even among his special occasion grades he never touches the Springbank, aged fifteen-years, unless he's drinking with his mother. He saves the very best for her. Today is a Springbank day. He raises his tumbler, toasts her, reaches over to her gravestone and clinks the crystal. Every night while she was alive they had a drink together. Sometimes it tasted watery so he knew she'd had a little during the day.

His mother always sat in the same chair. She was always sitting exactly there when he came home from the metal shredders. There was never anything in her lap. She was never doing anything. The TV was never on. She was sitting there waiting for him. He came home from work and walked through the door and there she was. Waiting all day perhaps. Perhaps not having done one single thing except wait for her son. She didn't change expression upon seeing him but her hands lifted to the armchairs and she began to push herself up from the cushions. She shuffled to the kitchen table, gathered her handbag and put on her coat and tied a scarf around her head, walked out the door and waited for him in the passenger seat of the car. After he cleaned and changed clothes, they drove over to the MCL Cafeteria. They were long-time regulars. His mother didn't even have to go through the cafeteria line. The tray bussers, older ladies themselves, picked her out something they knew she would like. Then they'd go home and have their drink, and sit just the two of them. He'd try not to feel lonely. Every night he'd think about Mary and the nine years they were married, and how he had let her down, how she had died, suffering, and how he had sold his soul to the devil.

On Thanksgiving he and his mother would eat at the MCL, and on Christmas Eve they were there early before it closed. It got so the people at the cafeteria were like his family. They came to his mother's funeral. He tried going back there after she died. There were some female regulars waiting to be his companions. But the people didn't seem like family anymore, or rather, they did seem like family but it wasn't comforting. He changed eating places and started going to a McDonald's. Night after night to the same one, and when they started to know him and greet him like one of their own, he went across the street to Wendy's, and then to a Burger King, and then to another McDonald's. He didn't deserve for anyone else to like him.

Worm liked to kid him. Had lots of nicknames for him. "Jet-setter" was Don Capachi's favorite. Made no sense. That's why he liked it. Worm asked him, "Hey, Jet-setter, wanna go to my hideaway and toke up?" Worm, that little boy-man who never listened to anyone, was about as close as Don Capachi came to liking someone again. He almost told Worm about Old Man Bonner, their boss's dad, the original owner. Sometimes, after a couple of drinks, he'd think someone ought to know. He'd be sitting alone in his house, his mother dead. If Worm had been sitting next to him, he would have told him.

He'd started up with the old man. Not many people knew that. *Bonner & Capachi,* that's nearly what the metal shredders came to be called. Don Capachi had been working as a musician. He played the clarinet. He played with a group of fellows first at church groups; then they moved up to the Deschler and Neil House. Downtown spots, everyone dressed up. Sometimes musicians traveling from out of state would board with him and his mother and they'd make a little money that way. One day one of the out-of-state musicians wrecked his car and left it on their front lawn and took the bus home. They were struggling to scrape together the rent so Don Capachi draped a *Parts for Sale* banner across the car and started selling it off piece by piece. He sold everything salvageable, the driver side door, the seats, the battery, the two tires that were still good. He put the unsold hubcaps in a box. With the money in his pocket he towed in another wrecked car and did the same thing. Eventually he had a parts emporium going, and it was paying some good side cash. The old man showed up one day, pretending to be searching for some hubcaps in a crate marked *Hubcap Heaven!* By then Don Capachi had a quite a collection going. By then as well their landlord had found out what they were doing, the yard they had ruined and the illegal business they were operating.

Old Man Bonner, he was sly. He seemed to know all about this angry landlord. He suggested leasing a regular spot and doing it right. They found a place together and ran a fence around it and put up a sign, *B&C Salvage.* Don Capachi operated it while the old man messed with his other businesses. After a while Old Man Bonner offered to buy him out, enough money for him and his mother to make a down payment on a house of their own. Enough money for him to get back to his music.

Of course Old Man Bonner wasn't an old man way back then. He had thick hair brushed up funny because of a cowlick. He seemed almost to have a limp but it was his fireplug build and the way he pushed forward in his stride as if his leadership forced him to power through wall after wall. After he was bought out, Don Capachi returned to his dream of being a musician. He was traveling some, still hoping to make it big. Old Man Bonner let him show up at the salvage yard and go on the job whenever he wanted. There was always work for a good grader and he was more than good — gifted, Old Man Bonner had declared him. In an indistinguishable pile Don Capachi could spot the grades of metal like notes on a staff. It gave him traveling money. In Missouri one night he met a woman named Mary. She was a singer in a family group, well-guarded by her brothers and father.

How anything worked was a mystery to him. But once love had worked for him. One night he had met Mary and something beyond him had acted in his favor. He didn't know how it had happened, so he had no idea how to repeat it. He never thought it would need repeating.

Across the road the two shirtless golfers finish the 16th hole. At the 17th green they wash their balls, then sit down on the bench and pop a beer. They pass it back and forth. Don Capachi watches them. How golf worked — just another mystery. He had watched it from this vantage point for ten years and he knew what was supposed to happen, but he didn't know how it happened. How the ball flew in the air and landed where you wanted it to land, how you chose what club to move you where, how you laughed or congratulated your partner or said *pick it up* or avoided the water. How you sat on the bench like those young men were doing now and felt so good about a job well-done you were reluctant to get up and finish.

How love had brought him and Mary together was as startling as walking up to those young men right now (limping, bent over, eighty-two years old), and choosing in their bags among all those metal sticks looking exactly alike, the right stick, and swinging it, the right way, and walking up to the green and finding that the ball had landed right where it should have. Once love had worked like that. But he didn't know how. He was ready to leave his forties, youth and promise way behind him, and it had finally happened, nearly a half century old and he had met Mary and somehow fought through the brothers and father guarding her, had somehow done and said the right thing and won her, and he thought that would be the final score, that he would be happy the rest of his life. When Mary died he knew it was over for him. He'd sold his soul to the devil to keep her well and it hadn't worked. Even if he knew how to fall in love again, God would never permit it.

Sometimes Worm took him to his secret spot behind the mountain stack of flattened autos. Don was small enough to inch through the tunnel, slow and careful, feeling his way along. Worm could do it at a trot. Worm had set up an extra chair for him. He took out his kit and set things up and Don found out what "toke up" meant. Worm thought he was introducing something new to him but the musicians knew all about that, they just used a different word. He much preferred his Islay malts. He took out his flask. About once a week he and Worm enjoyed themselves side by side. At night after those occasions he sat in his house or in a McDonald's and thought about it. He decided he was going to talk to Worm, tell him about the old man. Tell him the whole ugly business behind Bonner & Son Metal Shredders. Tell him as well about Mary. He was getting too old himself. There was no telling what might happen to him from one week to the next. He could die, and before he died, he wanted at least one person to know. He wanted to have a legacy out there.

Worm once asked, "Jet-setter, how come you always lived with your mama?" Don Capachi remembered saying something like "I was her only child," but the accurate thing to say would have been "I didn't live with her all the time. Not while I was married."

Worm would say, "Jet-setter, give me ten," and Don Capachi would list ten codes at random, *Ebony, Malic, Twitch,* and so on, the metals they corresponded to: red brass, old nickel, fragmentized aluminum. It was as easy as nursery rhymes, these codes. He had a natural talent that he'd just let die. He could have owned the business with the old man, not that he minded how it had turned out instead, Old Man Bonner in his leather chair and him at the punch clock. What bothered him was the cheap price his own soul went selling for. How easily he was bought.

In truth, he had been content doing low wage work, the grading and sorting work. It could be mindless or it could be mindful. It was music. Some days he was a composer; other days he was a listener. Either way the job got done and took nothing out of him. He went home to Mary. Every Wednesday his mother came over for dinner. Every Saturday they played cards. During those years he was glad he wasn't part owner. The job would have taken him away from Mary.

Then Mary got sick and his mother started staying over more. He'd come home and it was his mother waiting for him with a dinner she'd cooked, not Mary. Mary was sick in bed. Together they went up to the Cleveland Clinic and they said she had pernicious anemia. There was nothing to be done. Blood transfusions made her feel better. The doctors said the transfusions were just prolonging the inevitable. So why bother? they seemed to be saying. But so was life, he wanted to answer. Life itself was just prolonging the inevitable. So why live? Don Capachi told the doctors to keep giving her the transfusions. Keep giving the transfusions. The doctors said the insurance was going to stop covering them because they just prolonged; they only ameliorated, they didn't heal. But his Mary was like a vampire needing her blood, and he couldn't deny her. He put his house up for sale.

Old Man Bonner knew what was going on, of course he knew. He was at his best when his workers were sick and needed help. He gave Don Capachi, his old partner, all the time off he needed. He gave him a big Christmas bonus. He had groceries sent over; he arranged for a second opinion. He was good that way. If it had ended there, that would have been all right.

When the insurance was about to cut off the transfusions, Old Man Bonner came to Don Capachi with a problem of his own. The old man promised that if he helped him with his problem, he'd take care of Mary's transfusions out of his own pocket. Damn the insurance, she'd have the best care she could possibly have. The house wouldn't need to be sold.

He and the old man met a couple of times in the office after everyone else had gone home. There was a fish bowl on the desk. The old man liked fish. He was talking about building an aquarium into the wall. He had ideas like that. He was rich now. Don Capachi could have been rich along with him. But that had never mattered to him until now. Now he saw the one good use for money. When you had to make panicked repairs to your happiness, having enough money kept you from begging the wrong saviors.

The old man said somebody'd been hurting his daughter bad and now they had to get hurt. He kept talking about "they" so that Don Capachi imagined the mafia or a group of outlaws with bandanas masking their faces. He imagined how they must have left the old man's daughter when they were through with her. He didn't know how he, one man, strong admittedly, but just one man, could possibly take on a mob of them.

The old man said, "He needs the shinola wiped off his behind, you know what I'm saying now, right?" but listening to him, Don Capachi had no idea.

Eventually he realized they were talking about only one man and that this man was her husband. The old man said, "take a tire iron and whack him a few times." Before Don Capachi could catch his breath, swallow, and say I'm not killing anyone, the old man added, "Just knock the wind out of his sails, let him know somebody means business."

Don Capachi looked at the framed photo of Old Man Bonner and his wife and grown kids (one of whom was now the boss) and a couple of grandkids. Next to it was a framed copy of one of the old man's original sayings: *Your Metal Is Your Mettle.* The old man had a lot of pride. He had patriotism and didn't like long hair on boys. Don Capachi made himself ask, "What did he do?"

"Running with whores," the old man said. "He gave my daughter the clap basically, whatever they call it now. Now she's the one looks like the whore and word gets out even if doctors are sworn to privacy. I think he's going to have to give her a divorce and I don't think he'll want to ask her for any of her money either. I think he might want to go on his merry way with his overactive tail tucked between his legs. I think you might want to convey that message to him." The old man tapped distractedly on the fish bowl as he talked. He kept sprinkling in fish food. The next day all the fish were dead.

Don Capachi didn't mean for it to be Valentine's Day when he did the job, but the old man seemed extra-appreciative of his timing and slipped him a bonus twenty. Mary was in the hospital, her worst episode yet, and they were saying no transfusions absolutely not and all his sanity abandoned him. He didn't know whether it was rapture or madness he was feeling. He knew somehow the feeling preceded grief and that he couldn't afford to sit back and almost enjoy it, perversely enjoy the delirium. He waited for the husband late at night in the parking lot outside the Ding Ho Chinese Restaurant on Broad Street. "Whores inside," the old man had explained. First week of February they had sat in the lot one night so the old man could point him out. They waited almost two hours. "There he is," the old man said. "His name is Vernon."

Every day since that night Don Capachi had lifted the tire iron out of the trunk of his car and held it in his hands and wondered how he could ever swing something so heavy and lethal at a human being. He couldn't. He took a couple of socks and filled them with sand, and when Mary, dying, went into the hospital he found the will to swing frenziedly at the figure in the dark. When he struck the husband, the sock burst apart and sand nettled both their faces. He swung with his left arm and the other sock burst. Only then did he think to ask, "Are you Vernon?" The man started laughing even though he was bleeding. Even though Vernon was stunned and bleeding, standing upright but still and defenseless, he managed a laugh at the paltry little shadow of Don Capachi. He looked at Don

Capachi and Don Capachi felt Vernon's confidence. Vernon wasn't worried about this squirt with the two blown socks because he was bigger and heavier and meaner. And because of something else. The old man had warned him, use a tire iron because the asshole carries a knife. The man before Don Capachi jiggled his head, shaking out the stars, and with his chuckle dying down began to reach toward his pocket. Don Capachi struck out quickly with his bare fist. He knew how strong he was. His strength — what a surprise it was to this much bigger fellow. He struck again. He knew he would never play music again, not with what this man's hard bones were doing to his hands. It hardly mattered, something like that, not with Mary in the hospital, yet it was something he thought about as he continued to pound the man with his fists. The man was just a punching bag, no resistance. The sock, perhaps a silly idea, had at least prepared the way.

Mary wouldn't leave the hospital this time. The person waiting for him down the long hospital corridor was the old man. Not old then, of course. A vigorous man just tipping into his sixties. He'd come to offer support and sympathy. They walked down the corridor. Old Man Bonner's arm made it around his shoulder. The other hand slipped a twenty-dollar bill into his pants pocket. The nurses as they passed made no sound. The way their shoes stepped along lively and soundless was a comfort to Don Capachi, music's new passageway. He heard his own hard soles tapping along, scratching out the final defeat this time. His hands were bandaged and broken; he told the nurses he had beat them against a wall when the doctors had denied a transfusion.

He didn't realize he was being guided until he found himself pausing in front of a patient's room. He was pausing because Old Man Bonner was pausing. The old man came around to face him, as if they were going to talk, important, intimate talk that couldn't be done side by side while walking.

As the old man swung round to face him, Don Capachi turned to meet him and before he knew it he had walked into the patient's room and found himself standing at the foot of the bed. The patient's eyes raised in alarm, darted briefly to Don Capachi's hands, settled weepingly on the old man. Don Capachi thought, *I must have been kicking him too.* "Thought you'd like to meet an Italian friend of mine," the old man said.

Don Capachi felt crazed and dizzy as the old man made cheerful small talk before guiding him out so that he and Vernon could continue the conversation privately. He was left out in the corridor as the patient's door closed without a sound. The nurses came and went, passed him in the corridor. Everything was done without a sound. Mary died without a sound. Her brothers and father showed up in force, like a mountain clan. They took Mary back with them. They buried her in Missouri.

Across the road the golf course is empty. Don Capachi pushes in the last bite of the second hotdog. The shirtless golfers have left. He strains to see if there's anyone else out on the course. A straggler far out, playing alone. The countryside stretches like regular countryside, the flags invisible to his sight. He sits in the lawn chair. The sun is behind a cloud. He didn't bring a watch. It's warm enough to sit a while longer.

He should have told Worm. He should have told Worm the story. Who is left to tell?

Mary's father is dead now, and at least some of her brothers. Maybe all. She shouldn't be there in Missouri. She should be here with him. He'd like to hear what Worm would say to that. He'd say, "Jet-setter, go get her."

He's done with his job. Can't go back there anyway without Worm. He's been thinking about quitting for a long time. He gave it his life. He sold it his soul. He doesn't need to tell them he's leaving. He just needs to go. He'll go to Missouri. He has that left to do.

White's Lake

THE DIRT ROAD WAS NARROW and the way it rose erratically warned of a hill much steeper than the reality. The wild foliage along the shoulder, seldom attended to, brushed against the few passing cars.

Petr Kopecky stood at the top of the hill and watched the two women pull in. They had missed the dirt road on the first pass even though Lenka, the driver and anxious tour guide, was pressed close to the windshield to sharpen her vigilance. She had fretted in this posture for almost two hours; such startled draping over the steering wheel signaled something ominous or wonderful immediately on the horizon. It had caused ticks of adenaline in Brenda who was by now completely enervated by her role as passenger.

They retraced their route and found the dirt fork. It was no surprise that Lenka wasn't the kind of driver who would be attempting to guide the car up the dodgy path. They pulled into the scrappy turnout at the bottom of the hill. Lenka was slow to satisfy herself about the car's security as they unloaded. She stood and gazed at it as if giving the old Škoda a benediction or, more realistically, last rites, an impression reinforced by the caresses she gave the silver cross shining at her throat. Lenka was frail; prominent in her hands and bosom were dainty bones, the kind — Brenda imagined — that were bleached lighter than air. Brenda, in fact, had been afraid to give Lenka's hand a firm shake when they had first met. The young Czech woman seemed vulnerable to the point of painfulness and although the nicest person in the English department, the nicest person Brenda believed she had ever met, Lenka appeared to have few friends. She had attached herself to this weekend trip with a longing as transparent as her delicate constitution.

It was minutes before the women finally appeared from behind the bushes and trees. Petr Kopecky waved to them with a high sweeping arm, then marched down to intercept them. In case he hadn't known them before, the American of the two would have been easy to spot. She didn't keep her arms close to her; she let her body flair out. He took their bags and led them to his dacha. "Modest" would have been an inflated term for it. It was not much more than a hut. Its most appealing quality, suggesting childhood adventure, lay in the high stilts over the lake's shore. All around the perimeter of the lake were other dachas, some on stilts, some with their own docks. A few cottages looked rather grand, which took Brenda by surprise. Any sign of luxury or wealth was not only jarring, it seemed like a betrayal in this poor country, and she kept her own American standard of living well-hidden, choosing photos of homelife that featured tight shots with bland or walled backgrounds.

They walked under the stilts where it was sheltered and appealingly cave-like. The dacha covered them like a giant pitched tent. Petr pointed out the outhouse behind the dacha, a moldy square shed that sat at the summit of a sprawl of rocks and vegetation. The path up there was unscored by stepping stones. Brenda maintained her smile at the arduous journey required for peeing. "I really have to go," she said. She adjusted the handbag's strap from shoulder to over her neck and trudged off.

The small area inside the hut was both kitchen and living room. They pulled out chairs from the table set against the wall and faced each other in the manner of a group therapy session. Petr selected large glasses from the cupboard, otherwise filled with a reduced table setting of grandmotherly porcelain, and poured two big bottles worth of beer into them. They toasted quickly, without the usual fuss and cultural explanations the Czechs liked to give to Brenda. A silence fell as they drank. Brenda and Lenka had talked the whole ride. Brenda was tired from it. Lenka could go on talking but in front of a man so much her senior she was nervous and quiet. She was barely over thirty and Petr was in his sixties. He was one of those who had weathered the communists and seen his country through oppression and liberation. In the way he kept his personal life a nonexistent topic, he gave the impression of a man who owned as somber a history as his nation's — or simply a man habituated by necessity to erecting an unremarkable facade.

Lenka was old enough to have experienced a Czechoslovakia encompassing the Czech Republic and her own country, but young enough to have avoided much of the damage. On the ride Lenka explained her Slovakian family to Brenda, interrupting herself to point out scenery, and talked about going to England. She was Brenda's office mate for the semester. Petr, on the other hand, was someone who had just been friendly to her in the hallway, friendly in a way that was leisurely and almost priestly. He read and studied his books as if he lived in a monastery where nothing rewarded him except his own ethereal satisfaction. He had a wary yet placid expression that Brenda did not associate with the Czechs and their put-upon dourness. A cloud of gloom did not hang over him. He seemed contented.

The cleared space for their three chairs was not even big enough for a bed. Stacked against the walls were mounds of bedding material. Linen and yellowing lace topped every mound so that the clutter was sharpened into furniture. Brenda was sure she hadn't misunderstood about staying overnight, yet she couldn't figure where they would all sleep. A ladder stretched into an attic. It couldn't be up there. The ladder was too precarious and it led to a black hole.

A heavy banging on the door sent a dramatic spasm through Lenka. The beer in her hand jolted from the glass and splashed her face. Brenda reached out to rescue the glass before Lenka drenched herself.

Petr's expression didn't change. The man at the door spoke in a harsh rapid manner. He seemed to be having some kind of drastic problem. Brenda turned to Lenka but Lenka trembled in incomprehension, still too nervous to come to her senses. Petr stood silently while the man thrust his arms this way and that. After a long ranting sentence, Petr replied in a monosyllable. Brenda heard none of the enabling Czech exclamations that coached further expounding, not that the man's demanding rush of words needed prompting. Petr responded once again with a mild word or two, then shut the door. He turned back to them as though nothing had happened. His gaze was inward, as it must have been for so many years, walking to work, taking the train, eating, shopping, all these things under police surveillance. His calm meant he didn't notice things — Lenka's wet face, for example, and her need of a towel.

"Let's go eat," he said to them.

"What did that man want?" Lenka asked.

Petr shrugged.

Lenka was beset by worries. She was worried about her Škoda at the bottom of the hill, out of sight, out of hearing distance in case thieves sped away with it. On their way out of Brno, Brenda had tried to pay for gas, but Lenka refused to get more than a quarter tank because of possible petrol siphoning by the Ukranians.

Petr's tiny car was wedged into a semi-cleared space by the dacha's outhouse. He offered to exchange parking spots with Lenka. He drove them down the hill; they piled out then piled into Lenka's car. Petr maneuvered Lenka's car quickly up the hill while Lenka covered her eyes. It was all so odd and so much effort, even as Brenda was growing used to the surreal patina that coated the Czech logic. As her American colleague, on the way out as Brenda arrived to take her place, had said, "Kafka is starting to make sense, isn't he?" She had found Brenda standing almost literally open-mouthed in the hallway of what constituted the English department. Everyone's office was shut and bolted with two locks that had to be turned two or three times. The English department's main office door was also shut, and when she tried to open it with a key that didn't want to work, the secretary came to the door and said, "What?" Brenda had tried to keep her office door open and welcoming, but everyone passing by had shut it, including Lenka who then locked it.

Once Lenka's old Škoda was safely re-parked next to the outhouse, they walked down the hill to Petr's car. There was a noticeable limp in Brenda's stride that Petr hadn't noticed before. She wore tall leather boots with a thick heel that was quite high. She was as short as Lenka, but the boots made her taller and brought her up to average. That boost in height must have been worth a limp or two, Petr thought.

By now the strangeness of not being at the university was wearing off, replaced by a coziness. The three of them stayed together on the path. Petr looked at home here. His clothing was much the same as it was at the university: a short-sleeved gloomily patterned shirt in cheap material, and heavy pants that looked like they would sink and drown him if he waded into the lake. Solid across the shoulders, he still looked strong from his years of manual labor. A manual laborer, in fact, was what he looked like.

Petr drove them to a small restaurant that sat up high and looked over the curve of the village. They found a table outside where they had a panoramic view of the low mountains which were soft and dark green and melancholy. They had more beer and a round of fried cheese before the sandwiches came. Petr spoke to the owner with the same spareness of syllables he used with the man at the door. From his distant, succinct manner, Brenda and Lenka assumed they were strangers and were surprised when Petr told them the owner was an old schoolmate from grammar school.

Lenka, so obsessively talkative during the ride with Brenda, was still quiet. She wouldn't be so rude as to speak Czech to Petr with Brenda there. Besides, she was embarrassed about her Slovakian accent in front of a senior professor, even a senior professor the university was no longer friendly to. She was always trying to be a good host, and sometimes her wide smile felt heavy. She had chosen the seat with her back to the mountains so that Brenda would be sure to enjoy the view. She had nothing to look at besides the deck railing and the slope the restaurant cantilevered over. Mulch covered the slope in a careful gardening touch. Popping out of the black blanket were cabbage heads instead of flowers. Within the crinkled leaves she saw the face of her grandmother, and her fingers jerked to the scalloped edges of her cross. She found herself ashamed at being ashamed of the country accent she had inherited. She was even embarrassed about her English which was quick and entirely natural, but speaking it would upstage Petr. Petr spoke formally and slowly, with precise grammar and word choice. His English was perfect but it was from another time. Through no fault of their own, the senior professors didn't possess the colloquial English skills the students had come to expect. They had never been allowed abroad during the communist occupation and by the time of Václav Havel's velvet revolution they were too old. The students were complaining that the older professors had to go. Some of the professors spoke English worse than the students, especially the girls who like Lenka had taken au pair jobs in England to perfect their language skills.

This time when the owner returned, he and Petr acted like they knew each other.

"He wants to know how my mother is," Petr explained to Brenda. "He hasn't seen her for more than a fortnight."

Brenda said, "Your mother?"

"She comes to stay here every month. She's eighty five, she arrives by train, and he picks her up."

"That's nice of him."

"My mother put his tooth in milk when he was a boy."

He stopped for a swallow of beer. Brenda and Lenka attempted a satisfied smile.

"I knocked it out during football, and she put it in milk and saved it."

Brenda didn't understand this but she knew he hadn't misspoken. It was supposed to mean exactly what it meant. Unlike the other professors, Petr never asked her questions about arcane instances of English, questions she didn't know the answer to. Even the easy ones completely flummoxed her. They didn't make sense and even if they did, they were silly and not worth thinking about. She caught herself repeating their queries out loud until something sounded right, no doubt proving to them that her mastery of English was the cheapest form of inheritance.

Good morning — to you. Good morning — to you.

And the question: When *Good morning* is used as a farewell, is it necessary to attach *to you*? She had no idea. She had never used *good morning* as a farewell. It was something she'd only seen Maggie Smith do on the British screen. She had repeated the phrase in an uppercrust accent to see if that gave her any insight.

"This restaurant has very good beer," Petr said to her. "Drink."

"Your mother. Did we upset her plans?"

Petr shooed away the suggestion and handed her the beer. The owner came over and his gaze was on Brenda as he spoke to Petr. "He wants to know who you are," Petr said.

She gave a quick smile up at the man. "Ask him what tooth you knocked out."

The owner bared his teeth and pointed to the front one. It was true, Petr's mother had saved it. There was none of the darkening a dying tooth would have left.

A confusing vibration began to issue from the metallic electricity in the owner's teeth. In another second it pierced the dining room. The sharpening buzz spread to the surrounding hilltops far behind him, but from which hilltop wasn't clear. The sound was broader and more strident; it came from everywhere. A siren built to a climax, keening for attention. Then a man's voice started. They didn't bother with that disembodied woman's voice to soften the instructions. The announcements came over the tinny speakers placed throughout the village. Every day for decades the town had had to stand in attention and listen to the propaganda filling the air. While the Russian occupation was over, the ritual still played out each afternoon, although now the announcements were about things like garbage pick-ups and flu shots.

Petr acknowledged the screeching with a slight smile, the same sort of unperturbed expression that had once gotten him in so much daily trouble with the government. The police never seemed to like the way he went about his business in a contented manner that rendered them invisible and unfeared. Waiting in the train station at Mikulov one day, he was deep into his book and wished to keep reading. He let the first train to Brno pass and settled in for another hour of reading. The police approached and kicked the sole of his shoe when he didn't look up. They peppered him with questions and threatened to take him away. Why was he sitting here, why was he here, what was he doing, why he had purposely missed his train. *I wish to read,* he said and that was all he said.

It was early summer and the daylight lingered well into evening. They returned to the dacha with the intention of swimming in the lake. Petr pointed to the ladder spearing the dark attic. In fact, it wasn't an attic but his mother's bedroom. Brenda climbed the skinny ladder; at the top it was an awkward scoot to the flooring. Even for a former gymnast like herself, it was a little treacherous. Brenda could not believe that an eighty-five-year old negotiated this climb. She did not want to say anything until Lenka, too, complained how difficult it was. Petr handed up their bags and they dug out their swimsuits. Their bedrolls were laid out side by side, pressed together in the cramped space. Against the walls were small wooden boxes and bigger plastic ones holding the mother's things. The same needle-pointed lace hung over the stacks. A legless vanity and mirror sat like an altar. The area did not allow for standing up so they each wormed into their swimsuits on their backs, feet kicking the air. Brenda was not sure why they were here except that Petr had invited her and because she should take advantage of every cultural opportunity. Whenever she wasn't invited anywhere, she spent her four-day weekends traveling and staying in hotels without telling anyone. Initially worried that her Fulbright stipend wouldn't cover the costs, she had landed at a place where she could live like a king while the professors she worked with made five thousand dollars a year — less than a bus driver.

Beside the lake Lenka took off her necklace and laid the cross on a rock. Brenda was already in the water and watched her. Lenka's skin in the sun was a brilliant white; in the shade it was translucent over the pie wedge of tiny ribs that passed as décolletage. She was much more petite than the average Czech woman who tended to be tall, and in her swimsuit looked even more defenseless. Her hair was light blonde and delicate, lacking the sturdy straw color and texture that was more the norm. Although she was pretty, it was subsumed by her anxiousness, and she emerged a sexless, elfin creature. She was always smiling, offering herself in a tremulous way, so eager to be friends that it sometimes provoked a spasm of distaste in Brenda.

In the lake Petr swam over to Brenda and tread water. Brenda nodded toward an empty dock and the house behind it.

"That's a nice place over there," Brenda said. "I didn't expect it, to be honest."

"That was Mr. White's home," Petr told her. "This is White's Lake."

Now it made sense to Brenda, this suburban-looking ranch house. She had entertained thoughts of doing the same thing. What a vacation home she could afford here. "Oh! Was he American?"

"I translated the name."

"Of course."

"He was a Jew," Petr said.

Brenda said nothing because she didn't know what his next sentence would be. She'd been mildly shocked by some of her other colleagues and the sentences that had followed the word *Roma*.

"I stood in line with my mother when they took him away."

"Mr. White?"

He nodded.

She wanted to hear more but didn't dare intrude too much. "Not a cloud in the sky," she finally said, kicking herself at the diversionary comment.

"The sun faces a sad journey over this country," he said.

She always felt that she should respond to his sentences by naming the 19th century tome he was quoting from. Hardy, *Tess of the D'Urbervilles*? Collins, *Woman in White*?

It was The Book of Petr, no other book.

He made her feel lazy with her gift of English. It was like having natural beauty, giving to homely elders exposure to your youth and loveliness and thinking you should be thanked for it. Around Petr, Brenda had begun to think of herself as the sinner who understood sin by virtue of committing them and Petr as the spirit who watched and absorbed. This made her miss her family, those figures of flesh, yet she resented them and their flat incurious refusal to leave their routine and join her. She wondered how she would fit in when she returned. And she wondered how she would get through this night without a bathroom. Climbing down the ladder, then down into the night and up that slope: peeing would take half an hour and probably involve injury. Already Petr had told her not to go all the way to the outhouse unless necessary — just use the yard.

She swam away from Petr, peed in the lake, then headed to shore.

Lenka stayed in the water after them. She was busy playing a game in her head. She imagined one side of the lake as Slovakia and the other side the Czech Republic. Away in England, she had missed the '89 liberation. She returned to find her homeland divided into two. Now she was Slovakian, still a Czech legally but really no longer a Czech: please, a Slovakian with an accent that now identified her as non-Czech, a Slovakian, even lower than a Czech. No one would care or understand her identity crisis except a Slovak or Czech, and no one cared about Slovaks or Czechs except the Slovaks and Czechs themselves.

With her high-heeled boots tossed in a corner, Brenda's limp grew worse. It was not the high heel's fault then, Petr realized. He asked her about it. Brenda told him she had been a gymnast growing up. Last year she had taken her daughter to gymnastics class and got carried away, had charged down the mats into a roundoff back handspring. "You probably don't know those terms," she said. Petr, always surprising, turned around and mimicked a cartwheel and back flip. "When I landed," Brenda said, "my Achilles tendon — right here — snapped. It went up my leg like a tongue curling and stuck out from my calf."

Lenka features yawned in horror. "But you're so calm."

"Now. Not then!" Standing barefoot with a beer held aloft, Brenda loudly proclaimed, "I screamed my fucking head off, I'll have you know!"

A cry of shock and delight escaped Lenka at the forbidden word. Her hand flew to the cross at her throat, but the necklace wasn't there.

"The high heels help because the tendon is still short," Brenda explained to Lenka's sudden distressed chirps and whimpers.

"You must stretch it daily," Petr told her.

"I know. I do. It's getting better."

"Like this." Petr stood on the lowest rung of the ladder. He let his heel sink low into the stretch. Then he flew out his arm and free leg like a dancer, and posed for them. Brenda watched him. She could know everything there was to know on this earth and still not know as much as this man.

"I have to get my necklace!" Lenka grabbed a flashlight and started to leave. The door shook with a banging as she reached for the knob, and she leaped back into Brenda's arms.

The violent knock rattled the frame when it sounded again.

Petr opened the door to that same man. He was a big man. He had the Czech height and strong build. And he was angry. His hair was thick and hanging in his face, still dark brown against a creased middle-aged face. Brenda and Lenka huddled inside this hut that could so easily be blown down by a mad wolf.

Petr answered the man's questions, this time in longer sentences. The man grew harsher and continued arguing, but he was arguing with himself. Petr spoke to him in English before closing the door.

"Good night to you," Petr said.

Good night to you... Good night to you...

Was it a farewell or benediction or warning? And what did the *to you* imply?

Petr immediately opened another beer and began to pour it into their glasses.

The crazed knocking came again.

"Don't answer," Lenka beseeched him. Brenda was glad at this moment to have a frightened naif do the work for her.

Petr didn't look up when the knock came again. He poured the beer.

Lenka's hand had shot into Brenda's and Brenda was cradling it. They listened to the angry pounding. Brenda's own body thumped in panic, seeking flight from this place. All she wanted was to be gone.

"What's happening?" Lenka cried.

"He is on a journey and we are the next stop. He will leave."

"But what does he want?"

"He will leave," Petr said. "And go to the next stop. Like the sun."

It had been quiet for a long time. The man was gone. They had drunk more beers and Brenda had to pee again. They were sitting in their chairs. The three chairs were now arranged knee touching knee. They had pulled in close to help Lenka stop shaking.

"I need to get my necklace," Lenka kept saying. "He'll take it."

"He won't take it. He's gone."

"The water will wash it away."

"There are no waves here, Lenka."

"But the wind!" cried Lenka, the tears spilling.

They all walked down to the shore. Petr and Lenka stood under the tented stilts while Lenka aimed her flashlight over the rocks.

When she didn't find it at first glance, she walked from rock to rock and peered down with discouraged yips. The bright moon helped but then disappeared behind clouds and it grew blacker and the flashlight less useful. Petr and Brenda glanced at each other. It would be a long night if Lenka didn't find her crucifix.

This time the wail turned to delight. "Here it is!"

"That's fantastic, Lenka."

"It was on the ground. The wind blew it off the rock," Lenka explained victoriously. "The wind would lose it by morning."

"It's good we came."

"But we left the house unguarded," Lenka whispered.

"Yes, and now the monsters and chimera are inside."

"Don't say that, Petr," Lenka whispered.

But it was true. Standing under the stilts, Lenka and Brenda heard the noises. Lenka cried out in Czech, turned off her flashlight and palmed Brenda's beam. "He's up there," she warned. "Turn off your light!"

Brenda raised her head. She heard it, too. She dashed out from the stilts and caught a shadow at the window.

"Oh my god," she said.

"Did you see him?" Lenka pulled on Brenda's arm as if to pull out the answer.

"Yes, I saw him. I saw someone."

"No," Petr said.

"He's inside."

"No."

"Yes. He is. I saw him, Petr. I can hear him, too." Brenda advanced toward the lake, then stepped back under the hut's foundation. She slapped her forehead as she walked in circles.

"Did you forget I'm Czech?" Petr asked. He lifted a key. "I locked the door."

"Oh Christ," Brenda muttered. She was hugging herself. She

wanted to scream. She moved away from them to a dark corner. She grabbed one of the stilts for balance and pointed her flashlight up the slope. "I'm such an idiot," she said. "I'm an idiot who has to pee really bad. Thank god I'm not having my period."

But when her flashlight's beam illuminated the outhouse it illuminated the truth of what she had seen: the man was standing there, outside now, she could see him move into the outhouse and close the door and wait for her, tucked inside the square shoulders of this place everyone must go to eventually. Eventually they would all go there one by one and he would swallow them whole. The Czech language had contributed few words to America but it had given them *robot*, and that was what the outhouse had become, a robot, an outhouse that was wavering, now starting to move, a robot filled inside by this big angry wolfman.

She supported herself against a stilt until she caught her breath and the dizziness passed. She had already figured out how to outsmart the wolfman. She used a stilt for balance and the sliver of cover as she exposed her bare butt and squatted in the dark corner. Fortunately the beer had almost erased her self-consciousness.

"Do you need a tissue?" Lenka asked immediately.

"You're not supposed to see this."

"I can't see you."

"Whatever."

"What does *whatever* mean?"

"Whatever you want it to."

"Doesn't it hurt your leg to do that?"

"I'm fine, Lenka."

"Does it hurt?"

"Never. Only when I walk." The beer released Brenda's sarcasm, an American trait she had tried to leave behind.

There was Lenka's hurt silence, heavy in the dark.

"I'm kidding, it's fine. It serves me right for showing off."

"Showing off to your daughter, you mean?"

"To everyone."

"But you have a daughter," Lenka said.

"Yes. She's nine years old."

"You never told me."

"So what," she murmured. Brenda started to sigh, started to shrug. She let her shoulders slump. A moonglint off the lake revealed Lenka's shadow, slurpy and ill-defined. Her head hung down, melting into her chest. Lenka looked barely strong enough to keep herself standing. In the middle of peeing, Brenda fell on her butt.

"I'm sorry," Brenda said. "I haven't told anyone about my family. How would you understand? Why should you care about us? We're miserable people. We spend your yearly salary in a month and I don't know where it goes. It just seemed better not to let you know. How could you think we have problems?"

"We all have secrets," Lenka said. "I should have told you I am Slovakian."

"You told me twice in the car."

Lenka said nothing. The moon hit the lake again and the silence sharpened.

"You feel betrayed," Petr said to Lenka.

"You were going to be the first to know," Brenda said. "Lenka, I was going to tell you on the ride home. All about my family. It's something I can only tell a good friend. So naturally I was going to tell you."

Lenka's flashlight came on and she turned toward Brenda who was pulling up her pants.

"No no no," Brenda screamed.

Lenka laughed. "Let's not be angry with each other."

"I'm not angry with you," Brenda said. "Of course not."

"Because we're friends. And Petr, you're our friend," Lenka said, grabbing onto Petr's arm. "We're all friends, aren't we?"

Petr patted her hand calmly.

"We're safe," he told her.

"And we're friends," Lenka insisted.

"We will drink to that. Let's go inside and drink to that."

"Brenda?" Lenka asked.

Brenda could sense the tears welling behind Lenka's nervous laughter. "You're my friend, Lenka," Brenda told her. It was enough to stop the tears and it was just words after all, just words to be added to all the other words she had heard this day and not understood.

Digging the Hole

1992
Louisiana

Newly paved with two full lanes, the road caught her by surprise. In the thirties it had been a narrow dirt pike; for decades after, an oily gravel trail. When had this startling change come about? She could feel her Toyota spring into a surprised reaction. On this state-of-the-art surface it was hell-bent on setting a record. She let it fly, the only car on the road.

The radio she had ceased hearing miles ago broke through with an announcement: Stop!

Stop! the deejay screamed at her. Stop!

Instinctively she slammed on the brakes and jerked to a halt at the foot of a bridge. She turned off the radio but the same urgent voice persisted. Through the sun's harsh glare she could make out people milling on the bridge. They were workmen.

An enraged man began jabbing a spear at her windshield. His torso was naked and sweating. An orange nylon vest was pushed aside by a heaving belly. You almost hit me! he screamed. In fact, you *did* hit me.

She doubted that very much. In point of fact, the man looked fine. And his lungs were certainly in fine shape, as well as that part of the brain where filthy words resided. After an interlude of seething profanity to which she did not respond, he grew more infuriated and launched his spear at her windshield. Do you know what attacking a fucking state employee can get you! He grabbed the spear again and brandished it threateningly. Now she saw that the spear was actually a sign. She recognized its red octagonal shape as well as the four white letters. His screams dripped salvia as he helped her spell it out:

S. T.

O. P.

S. S.

H. —

He wasn't near finished, though she was past listening to a spelling bee. He braced the sign like a crowbar and made a menacing gesture toward her windshield. I'm gonna fucking break—

Abruptly he halted. That was it; his tirade was over. He shook with the effort of stopping himself, but stop he did. The last of his curses spent themselves in a long cough. He raised his hand in apology. Sorry, he managed to hack out. Just be careful, ma'am, okay? He limped back to the foot of the bridge (a limp! what fiddle-faddle melodrama, she hadn't even been close!) and took up his position, leaning on the staff of his stop sign. He kept clenching his neck muscles and mouthing words through a penitent grimace. No doubt he believed his shocking behavior and language were going to cause her immediate death by stroke. In her eighty-four years nothing so horrible as this had ever happened to her and yes, she could feel it coming on now, an explosion inside her aged head, a fatal collapse induced by one man's savage epithets...

The credit some people gave themselves.

It was irritating, to say the least. Here she was making good time on a good road and now she was stuck at the foot of this bridge, a tiny bridge spanning a trench of swampy water. Why expand a road into two lanes if the bridge on that same road was going to remain a single choked slot?

Why?

A good question for a lot of things.

Worse, she was idling in a spot that caught the direct sun. She drummed impatiently on the dash as she waited out the family crossing the bayou from the other side. Taking their biblical time about it, too. A rusty truck with an brood riding in the open bed trundled over. Saran Wrap for the passenger window, no less. They smiled and waved to her as they passed. The Dust Bowl is over! she tried calling to them, but she couldn't get the window down in time. She was pressing the wrong power button. The side mirror bowed, providing her with a view of the fresh asphalt.

After a few moments she became aware of a tapping noise. The man of many threats was timidly applying knuckle to window. He was motioning that she could go. It's your turn, he said. He smiled encouragingly. Must have abused his granny at some point, trying to make up for it with her. He was solicitous now; he wanted to be helpful. He had twenty or thirty blond strands on the top of his head and no hat to shield the August rays. His bare shoulders and the tips of his ears were alarmingly red. He wouldn't be alive much longer if that kind of sense played out in the rest of his life.

Now the man seemed on the verge of obliging her with a little push, as if this were a toy she was driving, not a real live Toyota. She gunned the motor, letting him know what kind of horsepower he had barely escaped (a limp!). He leaped out of the way and landed on his derriere. Let that be a lesson to him: her foot might be ancient but it could step on the gas as well as the next person.

The Toyota jumped onto the narrow bridge and knocked against the railing. Good Japanese thoroughbred that it was, it straightened out almost immediately.

The water crept murkily on both sides of her.

Louisiana.

She now came to this state at most once a year and was glad to leave. She had in the past held good memories of her trips, and the shadows didn't bother her. The more darkly the bayou gleamed, the happier it had made her. That's who she was. Too late to apologize for it.

Beyond the bridge another man with a stop sign was also leaping out of her way. The Toyota shivered in a fishtail as it spun off the gravel shoulder onto the macadam. The back fender might have nudged the fellow. No harm done. She could swear it was the same man. Looked just like the other one. Same orange vest, same burning shoulders, same jutting stomach with tributaries of perspiration. She drove on.

Sometimes she used to pass prisoners on this road, docile and slow-moving. The heat shimmies broke them apart as she passed.

Lately the days hadn't been too good to her. A deep ache in her bones awakened her throughout the night. By morning her throat was ragged, her eyes encrusted from the pain, and she found herself lying in bed regretting things: Her son Leonard. A husband who had deserted her. The way the headlights of her Packard had broken through the mist and landed on a little boy, the buttons of his velvet coat fastened up to his chin.

But today was not one of those times. Today was a run-over-whoever-gets-in-the-way day. Finally, a good day. The man with his death threats and swinging stop sign had been the silver lining in the cloud. He made her realize she was the same person she had always been, Mrs. Jarmilla Price, a woman who had successfully accomplished what needed doing without ever having to resort to vulgar words.

Up ahead was the little white church where she used to stop for her final business with her new charges. When she saw it, she pressed on the accelerator. It was only a few more miles now to the leper farm. She hurried past the lonely parish: no reason to stop this time.

The road was deserted. The car plunged into tunnels of huge shade trees. It was 1992, but except for the air conditioning and the spongy soundless roadway under her and the fact that she wasn't pregnant, it could have been 1934.

1934
Louisiana

Their first job for her was a little boy. When she arrived with him at the leper farm, the child seemed almost content. No tantrums even though he was spoiled rich and none of his Christmastime presents came with him. They said it was the first child who hadn't arrived crazed with weeping. They asked her how she did it. She fought against the vanity her husband had always berated her for and shrugged in a way she hoped looked both humble and mystical. A woman's touch, was all she allowed.

Autumn, 1964
Texas

The first thing Jarmilla hated about this girl living in their home was her name: Penny. There were many more important things to dislike about her, but if for a moment Jarmilla happened to forget about these, the silly name brought them all back. Penny. Parents too cheap to buy her a decent name. Jarmilla could testify to that. She'd dealt with those parents years before.

The girl was actually sleeping in Leonard's bedroom (that her son was away on an oil rig was a minor point). For all intents and purposes the girl was already her daughter-in-law, having ensnared Leonard with a vacuous prettiness. But she was more than just a bad penny underfoot. The face was a constant reminder of the job Jarmilla had done fifteen years earlier. Surely Penny, no matter how dull-witted, had noticed that a member of her family, her own twin sister in fact, had gone missing one fiery night?

It was in 1949 that the smooth transactions had come to an end. Jarmilla had her first live wire: a leprous farmer's daughter she had to chase through a skimpy cornfield. If the father had worked like a proper farmer to grow a better crop, Penny's sister might have escaped in the taller, thicker stalks. It would have been a harsh blow to Jarmilla's ego to see one get away, but god how she now wished the girl had succeeded. For the live wire had returned in the coinage of her twin. Life indeed was a vicious circle.

Jarmilla and Penny found themselves alone while Leonard was gone. The girl's eyes were always following her, mostly confused, sometimes scared, but it was the one thing Jarmilla didn't mind. The stare helped her to think of a plan. One day over supper Jarmilla observed Penny's brain once again go fruitlessly to work. This time Penny seemed to have gotten as far as recognizing that she'd seen Jarmilla before.

You're wondering, aren't you? Jarmilla said, pushing away her salad.

About what? Penny asked.

How many sisters do you have?

Three.

Four, isn't it?

Three, Penny said.

I guess with all those girls your mother didn't mind giving one up.

Penny blinked rapidly at her.

You used to have a twin sister, Jarmilla said.

Penny's head lowered.

Whatever happened to her, I wonder? Jarmilla taunted.

I don't know.

Oh I think you do.

Penny wouldn't answer.

I used to have a job. It involved people like your sister. I came and got them. Don't you remember? You've seen me before. That night I chased down your sister.

The girl's brows lifted furiously. She opened her eyes wide to block any reaction, but still the tears came.

Never had a parent say no once they heard the name of the disease. Penny picked at her food.

I would never have let Leonard go, but I didn't blame the parents. Did you blame your parents?

The tears dropped even as the girl shook her head.

Do you want to see your sister? Your own twin sister?

More tears before the girl raised her head and glanced at Jarmilla in a fit of scrutiny. Jarmilla noticed a rush of blood in that wan nothing of a face. She saw the girl trying hard to get her brain to click on the memory. Perhaps Penny had been looking out the window in the dark when Jarmilla had gone on that footrace through the cornfield. Fifteen years had passed since the last time Penny had seen the mirror image of herself in the flesh, as a howling figure in the night.

Were you watching us?

Penny's chin pushed into her chest in a odd contortion.

Stop that! Jarmilla scolded. I couldn't live with myself if I were you. Do you think I would have given up my son just because he was a leper?

It was infuriating the way the girl went blank and wouldn't answer.

However bad you think I am for taking her away, the ones who let her go were worse.

That's not nice, Penny said.

I wouldn't have given up my own flesh and blood. You've already proven that you will. I'm the only one Leonard can count on for loyalty.

Blank, blank, blank.

You're no good for him. You're just one of these I say jump and you say how high persons. If they came to get Leonard, you'd just wave good-bye.

Who would come to get Leonard? the girl asked.

Anyone!

Blank again. How she wanted to slap her!

You'd just wave good-bye.

No I wouldn't, Penny sniffled.

But you don't mind him risking his life to put an extra carat in your ring. Jarmilla felt her hands begin to shake as her anger grew. Leonard had gone off to work on an oil rig to make money for the marriage. It was dangerous work and here the girl was all for it. Not a moment's pause at the high fatality rate in that kind of job. Or the loneliness, or the sea sickness, or the type of men he'd have to fraternize with. Meanwhile, as each day Leonard risked life and limb, Penny rested contentedly in their home, eating their food, not working, not at all. Sat, only that, all day — just like her father on his tractor. She slept in Leonard's room, and it was as bad as if Leonard was in there with her. The trespass ate at Jarmilla. Your sister put up a fight. I can't see you doing that.

Penny pushed at the lettuce on her plate — languidly; the hands weren't even trembling. Once again Jarmilla had to control the urge to reach over and smack her. She said, I'll take you to your sister if you promise to leave my son and forget all about him and this nonsense about an engagement, forget he was ever born, that you were ever here. Just leave us. You've made a wreck of things.

The words were as close to a blow as Jarmilla could make them. She cleared her throat harshly to bring the girl to attention, and offered her this bargain: the sister for her son. She saw that the father's lazy veins ran through Penny. Doing nothing left her completely satisfied. No passion dams would burst if her beloved fiance were taken away.

So unlike the live wire in that respect. Penny's twin was the one Jarmilla was unable to forget. In all those years a thirteen-year old had been the one to score her mark. Her pudgy hands, when

Jarmilla caught her and pulled her through the stalks, slapped at her with a powerful heat. The palms were hot as live coals; they were actually blistering her. The girl fought like crazy, the only one, strangely, who had ever fought. The family house stayed dark, pretending not to hear.

As strong as the live wire was, Jarmilla was stronger. She roped her up like a calf and set to dragging her through the stalks. When she got to the car Jarmilla looked back: the cornfield was on fire. She could hardly drive for the burns on her hands. Fifteen years later she still suffered weekly fears that the girl had infected her.

So, she asked Penny, what is your choice? She knew Penny would want to see her twin, that her love for her sister was stronger than her love for Leonard. For loving her sister was like loving herself.

They packed their bags and loaded up the car and made their drive into Louisiana. The Beatles were on the radio, incessantly. "I Wanna Hold Your Hand," crackling up and down hills. It made the girl happy so Jarmilla kept it on, but all the song brought her was the sight of that burning cornfield and no explanation yet in her life about its meaning. They stopped at a motel, and Jarmilla paid extra for separate rooms. Through the curtains she watched people splashing in the motel pool. Several transistor radios lay on the cement around the perimeter, all of them tuned to the same station, the sound like flashlights beaming together from different points. She had remembered to bring whiskey and poured herself a glass. All day long listening to that song by that foreign invasion wearing long bangs.

Then she noticed Penny sitting in a lounge chair at the pool, snapping her fingers as if she were part of the group and their transistors. A silly girl, as silly as her name. With one cent for brains.

Girl. Yet the girl was almost thirty years old. And still behaving like this, like a junior miss trying to make new friends.

It was early afternoon the next day when the little white church came into view. Jarmilla slowed and pulled in, and bounced up the dirt path. She reached over and turned off the radio. The church was shuttered up tight. Now get out, she said.

Are we here? the girl asked stupidly.

Well almost, she snapped. Now you need to stretch your legs before we arrive. I want to show you something.

She could feel the whiskey at the back of her head, a cottony throbbing. Leonard had always been faithful about bringing her washcloths when the headaches got bad. He'd pull the drapes, but sometimes even twilight was too bright for her eyes. She'd soon vomit in the toilet, and in the midst of retching, the bolts of pain cracking across her temples would make her fear she was having a stroke. After all, she was fifty-six years old.

Penny was strolling in the weeds around the church. Jarmilla examined the ground as she walked, her foot scraping out half circles. She called sharply to the girl.

This was their last stop before they died, she told Penny. I chose this place, here at a churchyard, before God.

Before depositing them at the leper farm, Jarmilla let each of her bounties experience the death and rebirth her religion had taught her. They were lepers. They were dead now. Those who had loved them had ceased to love them. Their chair at the table was not empty, it was simply not there anymore. Their name would never be spoken again by anyone they had called Mother or Father or Friend. Did they understand? They were dead. Now they would be born again at their new home but would remain as nothing for the rest of their lives to the world outside.

After telling them this, she made them dig in the ground by the church, and they cast their old selves into the hole and recited the prayer she taught them.

Here was one of the places we dug, she told Penny. I can still see it. I still remember the boy. A wealthy one looking just like Little Boy Blue. It was a mansion I drove up to and they waited on me like royalty. Would you like me to teach you the prayer?

Penny shook her head fearfully. She was looking at Jarmilla the same way they had all looked at her. Terror in their eyes, but acceptance. They were listening to a ghost story about themselves.

They knew they were the devil's own, you see, she told Penny. They knew I was telling them the truth. That's all I ever tried to do.

The girl began to cry. Jarmilla ignored her. She said, One thing I didn't tell you. You're going to need to disguise yourself. They'll see that you're family. You look just like her.

How do you know? the girl slobbered.

You're twins, aren't you? If they suspect you're a relative they'll never let you in.

She let the girl go on weeping. She didn't tell her that she had been visiting her sister every year for the past decade and a half.

1992
Louisiana

She emerged through a tunnel of shade trees into the sudden glare. Fortunately the road had remained deserted, for Jarmilla was now on the other side, and her trusty Toyota was spinning around. Her eyes were still shut against the abrupt dagger of the sun.

The car stopped spinning. No harm done. She let her eyes adjust for a few moments, then continued on. She realized after a mile or so, when she noticed how well the trees were protecting her from the sunlight, that she was going the wrong way. She tried turning around in the road. Her front wheel sank into a ditch just as the three-point swing was nearing successful completion. She applied the brakes, then the emergency brake, then could do nothing but wait.

She kept the motor running and the air conditioning on. After a few minutes a good ol' boy's pickup came roaring down the pike. It squealed on the brakes but streaked well past her before the truck could get itself to stop. Without a second's hesitation — in fact, the pick-up was still rocking — the driver and passenger jumped out, ran over and took positions at the front of the car. With a flick of their husky bodies she was jolted back onto the road, pointed in the right direction.

They were used to this, it seemed. Well, all of Louisiana was a ditch when you came right down to it.

The boys spoke as fast as they moved and when she thanked them she had no idea what they replied. They jumped back into their pick-up and were out of sight so quickly she wondered if she hadn't been seeing a mirage. She hadn't even had time to get out of her car. Barely enough time to find the right button to get her window down, but it hadn't mattered since she'd had no idea what they'd said to her. A couple of friendly hillbillies, that was all.

Before taking on the road again she fumbled in her hand-bag for sunglasses. They were the ridiculously large goggle kind the ophthalmologist had prescribed for her. An outright embarrassment to wear, for they fit full over her regular pair as daintily as a welding shield. For heaven's sake, they were some-thing only an albino would have such need of.

Well, if they were going to get her where she was going she would wear them, and she would wear them cheerfully. Something came to her: her optimistic disposition had always pleased her.

As if to verify this, a car honked and pulled up beside her. Everything all right? the driver shouted.

Fine, she called over with a satisfied smile. Just locating my sunglasses. Doctor says I need them.

Better get a move on before you get hit.

I plan to, she said. As soon as you finish your speech. She cocked her head over the steering wheel, yanked the gearshift around from

Park to Neutral to Reverse to Drive, then sped off with a laugh and her optimistic nature intact.

The last few miles were incident-free. She could do this drive in her sleep.

She was here.

The leper farm looked like a grand plantation. A perimeter of clapboard buildings enclosed a courtyard within. The outside walls of hospital and rooming houses gleamed a medicinal white. But the paint was pocking now, she noticed. The place had lost some of its grandeur. It felt smaller, too. As she walked into the main building, she cleared her throat several times to wipe the smile off her face. She had always loved the moment of her entrance when the guard got halfway through a question before checking himself and bowing in recognition. A murmur would filter immediately throughout the main hall, and then magically the director would be there to welcome her personally. The director was a spinster who always wore a severe-looking skirt and mannish type of dark jacket. Everyone else, the nurses, the cooks, the housekeeping staff, wore hospital whites.

This time no security guard was posted to ask her to state her business. The people she did see were dressed in street clothes. The place might have been some business school she was entering. A business school languishing between terms, for few were about.

Now she knew what was different about the place. She walked back outside to double-check. Unbelievably, the barbed wire fence was down. The long line of cement garages that housed the hospital vehicles stood gaping and empty. The stucco had dropped off the walls in large chunks, turning the garage wall into an ill-completed jigsaw puzzle.

Hello, Jarmilla.

Jarmilla turned to find someone almost as old as she was. Still wearing her nursing whites, Nurse Cora had shrunk into its starched shell. A good third of her had evaporated. Such a rapid deterioration since last year. No, since the year before that or so.

Things have changed, Jarmilla said.

Oh my yes.

She waited for Nurse Cora to explain. When there was silence, Jarmilla snapped, Well, what?

Well? Well, it's 1992. Did you ever think 1992 would come around? I didn't. Cora jerked into a coughing fit.

Are you sick? Jarmilla asked.

Everyone is sick here. Sick or dead.

Jarmilla tapped her foot impatiently.

We're closing down, Cora said.

Let me speak with the director immediately.

Oh, she's one of the dead now.

Jarmilla felt a spat of dizziness, then realized she had been standing all this time in the hot sun. Cora followed her back inside, where the high ceiling and floor of Spanish tile gave off a cool draft. Jarmilla removed her monstrous sunglasses. Folding them in her hand, her fingers could barely wrap around them they were so big.

Cora sighed. Times have changed. It's 1992 already and I'll soon be eighty.

You said that already!

Did you know leprosy is not considered contagious these days?

That's foolish, Jarmilla said irritably.

We've been closed for a year and a half.

The large sunglasses in her hand felt very heavy. She looked down. A smokey glass brick, too heavy. Her hand dropped to her side.

Cora bent over, inched her shrinking body down and reached for the glasses that had fallen to the floor. They went skating across the tile. Jarmilla got them herself. She gripped them tightly. Closed, she gasped.

Yes.

But... Where have they gone?

I don't know. They just... melt away. Cora whispered melt as if the word itself were dissolving on her tongue.

Some have been here for fifty years.

At least.

Are there any left? Jarmilla said.

Oh, lots, Cora said. All the old ones. Me, too. Nowhere else to go. What am I to do, Jarmilla?

Why are you thinking of yourself at a time like this? Jarmilla grunted in disgust. Really, Cora. You don't have leprosy. There's no excuse to find yourself in this situation. Where's your family?

Cora shrugged.

You have your funeral arrangements made, don't you?

At my age? Of course.

Well? Then that proves you can think ahead when you want to. You must have known retirement days were coming.

What about you, Jarmilla? Are you still... independent?

You can say it. Thank you, I'm still very much on my own, living in my own house. No assisted living for me yet.

As ornery as ever, too, Cora said.

And just as independent. Look how healthy I am.

And your son?

Why I see him every day, of course. See how it helps me stay young. Look at you. You were always too proud of being small. Now you see where it's taken you. You're withering away.

Is he still a judge? Cora asked slyly.

Who?

Your son.

You know quite well he's a lawyer.

Thought he might have been promoted by now.

He's not a drunk and he doesn't like whores, so he can't be bribed. No one has use for a judge like that.

And your grandchildren?

Very well, thank you.

And is he still a lawyer?

Who? Jarmilla demanded.

Your son.

You've asked that! Is he going to change near age sixty and start driving buses?

And is he still the very best one in the city? Cora's ailing chuckle was nonetheless laced with calculation.

Why do you put words in my mouth! Who would know such a thing! Is there a plaque that announces the best in the city? I merely said he was very good at what he did. And I said it once, years ago — years ago, Cora! — and left it at that. I suppose yours might be the best at something, too.

Cora's gaze abandoned Jarmilla for the empty air. I don't know where mine went. Her feeble voice trailed off.

I'll speak to the new director now, Jarmilla stated.

None to be found. We're closed.

Jarmilla turned to leave Cora.

But *she's* still here, came the whisper behind her.

Jarmilla wheeled round. I've never liked your particular brand of humor, Cora. And your little tricks. I might as well get it out of my system. You can do me no more favors now.

She's here. Cora smiled shrewdly.

No! It's not possible. She would have been the first to go. That girl! This barbed wire fence had trouble enough holding her in.

Cora laughed weakly but with evident pleasure. Her throat gurgled in an ugly way. This time Jarmilla didn't turn back even as Cora tried to call something to her. She crossed into the open courtyard. The fountain was dry, but it had been the last time she was here. She ducked around the pillars into the open-air hallway and, using her annoyance for strength, marched to the room.

1934

Oklahoma

Their little squatter's house was wrapped snug against the blowing dust, but it pooled in the bed at night. Her hands roaming for her husband found fingers of dirt under his pillow. Where is he? My husband hates me. Why? Why?

The dust was everywhere. The windows were shuttered and blanketed, but the dust awaited her in the cereal bowls locked inside the cupboard. She thought she might not live through it, the false darkness, the nearest friend far away. She longed to hear her husband call to her. Jarmilla?

One time he didn't come home. They found his Packard Studebaker. They never found him. Her self-righteous Christian neighbors believed that playing with God's scourge had brought her husband to this hidden end. Even in the midst of the Depression the lure of money couldn't overcome the fear of touching one of them. It was true, her husband stole children and wives and brothers and sisters, but they didn't understand that someone was needed. Someone had to do it. He would get the calls, late at night it always seemed, as if he were a doctor or a priest, and then he would be off, leaping states to find them, gone for weeks at a time.

At first her husband was frightened by what he did and then completely charmed. No one came after them, he marveled. No one searched, trying to steal them back; no one followed after them; no one ever did; even the indispensable mothers were forgotten.

Now something had claimed her husband and he was gone. Or he had been charmed into claiming himself and staking out a new life where no one would follow him.

Each night the blowing dust made visibility a laughable dream. She needed to see to begin to look. How could she hope to find him?

She called the leper farm, called them often, and lied that she had often done her husband's work for him because of his trouble with liquor. One day they called her back and said there was someone who needed picking up, that perhaps this required a mother's touch. She drove through the night. Through a fog that cloaked the morning in cold rings of darkness, a mansion like a castle emerged. She drove up a half-moon drive where a maid awaited her with a millionaire boy. He was dressed in a velvet Christmas coat buttoned up to his throat. His chin was lost in it. Where am I going? he asked in a small voice. In the back seat the little boy squeezed himself into a ball trying to believe the maid's lie. Jarmilla never spoke to the boy except hours later when they arrived at the little white church and she realized her religion had called her in a further instruction. On the front seat beside her was an infant. She'd lost her first son to whooping cough.

Anybody can forget anybody, her husband had said.

Autumn, 1964
Louisiana

She watched Penny take in the sight of the leper farm. The girl gaped at the barbed wire fence. Why it's a prison! she wept.

They're lepers, Jarmilla explained. Get control of yourself.

When they walked into the entrance building, she had Penny sit in a corner while she dealt with the guard. It was the first Negro one she had seen, and he didn't know her. Before he could call the director, it was no surprise that Nurse Cora walked by. Her bad timing was impeccable. Jarmilla! Cora greeted warmly, but the warmth seemed heated by mockery. She saw that Cora was dyeing her hair a few shades too dark, and it brought out her age and the new wrinkles that went along with being nearly fifty. Cora was one of these dainty people, used to being cute. Cute and useless. In her day Jarmilla could rope a steer, and it had come in handy.

Jarmilla arranged her voice in a greeting. Cora! How pleasant to see you. I'm here for my visit. But I'll see the director first.

She's gone.

Jarmilla checked her watch. It was her luck to arrive at lunch time. She was still thinking of how to introduce Penny. She would say the girl was her son's fiancée and had heard about her line of work and was filled with admiration and fascination.

Does she have a usual hour? Jarmilla asked.

The director? Cora asked.

Yes the director, Jarmilla said, trying not to show her irritation. Cora loved to play these games.

Oh the director's eating lunch at her desk today. I hear they're building a restaurant not two miles down the road.

Then I'll see her after my visit. Jarmilla put authority in her voice. Cora liked to argue, though she played a character lost in a riddle. Cute and dainty. She had fooled a lot of people, but not her.

She's gone.

Really, Cora!

The Negro guard stepped over. She trying to tell you—

Then why doesn't she just tell me.

We had ourselves some escapees, the guard finished.

For a moment she was stymied by his locution and could only picture the guard having himself some chicken. Then she understood what he meant. Not again! she said.

It seemed to her that Cora stifled a laugh.

I must see the director, Jarmilla said.

We were going to call you. She thought you might have some notion of her whereabouts. Since you two are so close, Cora, not surprisingly, enjoyed adding.

Should be easy enough to spot a leper girl, Jarmilla wanted to say, but it was not the case. The girl's leprosy had not progressed much and she wasn't disfigured. Jarmilla walked away from Cora and the guard. She left Penny sitting in the corner and went to the staff powder room. She sat on the toilet and thought. She felt one of her headaches boiling up.

1963
Iowa

She and her boy Leonard traveled through the farm communities selling cooking ware. In the cities they had fared poorly, but these rural outposts were gold mines. They were a good team. There was always someone willing to host a cooking party. It was a good excuse to get far-flung neighbors together, and the host received free gifts. Jarmilla would stay in the host's kitchen and cook while Leonard worked the living room, describing the magical qualities of all the roasting pots and double-boilers and time-saving implements.

In the city only the old crones would show up, tight with their money and unimpressed. But here in the country it was a regular bachelorette festival. Oh, and how the girls loved Leonard! He looks like John Kennedy! they would squeal. And how they loved to spend their money, as if that was the key to everything, throwing it to the wind for pots and pans and then next their golden honeymoon and an enchanted life far away from cows. By the time she pulled the cake out of the oven, most of their wares would be sold and the girls laughing would draw straws over who got to marry Leonard. He was a fine, God-fearing boy and he never let the obvious show, that he could do much better than any of their type, which was part of his charm. He was going places, anyone could see that.

It was only when that girl showed up at one of the functions that some curse that had always been circling finally settled upon her. She was caught up in their success, didn't think that girls would come all the way from the next town over (a town in name only since nothing was there). Jarmilla recognized her as soon as she walked in, for she had been visiting that same face for years. For a moment she thought it was actually the live wire herself. There had already been two escapes.

Afterwards Leonard said they should stay over in the town for a week. The demand at this party had well exceeded the supply they had on hand. He sent her to get restocked in Des Moines. Jarmilla already knew what she would find when she came back.

And then soon Leonard was saying he wasn't making enough money, that he had to do something else. It's because of her, isn't it? she asked her son.

And then the girl with that terrible silly name that suited her bankrupt personality just perfectly, showed up one day at their doorstep and him soon packing for the oil rig. He invited Penny to stay in their house while he got money enough for their marriage. There was nothing at all to this girl, but Leonard kissed her good-bye like something out of the movies.

Autumn, 1964
Louisiana

Nothing at all to the girl, Jarmilla thought as she sat on the toilet. And yet Leonard behaving this way, ready to throw away his future. He was bewitched. She wondered if she hadn't seized the wrong girl on that night fifteen years ago. The strangeness of that one had always lingered. Strange that she had been the only one to put up a fight — the only one — and maybe there was good reason. Maybe she wasn't a leper after all. In fifteen years she had hardly showed any outward symptoms of the disease. This other one though, Penny — she had a cheapness of blood and brain and personality that did her name justice, yet, too, the devil's power to bewitch.

It made sense. Somehow she must have intuited it all along. Hadn't she stopped at the church with Penny and virtually enacted the same cleansing ritual? Hadn't her sister been the only one who had never visited the church? Jarmilla believed at the time that it had been because this wild one was too dangerous to let out of the car, but no, she realized now.

The cornfield on fire had been trying to tell her this.

She left the powder room and her heels tapped a loud message on the tile floor. Penny still sat in the corner, playing the fading movie star, a scarf tied under her chin, round tortoise-shell sunglasses hiding her eyes. Jarmilla walked into the director's office and sat down.

The director looked up from some brew she was stirring in her cup. You heard, she said.

Her voice was thick with congestion. She patted the sides of her man's haircut with the palms of her hands, a gesture Jarmilla remembered from other visits. Her jacket was the same style as all the other jackets Jarmilla had seen over the years, exactly like a man's jacket except clearly a woman's. For years Jarmilla had been trying to figure out her clothes and where they came from. They didn't look handsewn.

Now don't look at me like that, the director said. We did our best to keep her in. We can't exactly resort to chains in 1964. I imagine she'll be back. It might be a few years.

What did you expect, letting her roam the woods like that free as a bird?

For the first time she seemed happy, the director said. And it helped the fire department.

It helped the fire department, Jarmilla repeated.

I mean the police department. The director checked Jarmilla's reaction. Now don't look at me like that. It helped train their dogs.

As if they needed a leper girl. Nobody else can run through the woods?

People are afraid of those dogs. She loved them.

So she trained them until she could outsmart them, Jarmilla mused out loud, hoping one of her arrows might penetrate the director's thick skull. Or else one of those policemen fell in love with her and helped her get out. My god, I bet it was a regular brothel out there under the trees. I'd say you got what was coming to you.

Her speech over, Jarmilla let out an exasperated sigh, but it was more theatrical than real. She leaned back, her headache receding. She always felt superior to these mannish spinsters with nothing but their careers to watch them go gray. Because here she was, Mrs. Jarmilla Price, having loved, married, mothered, succeeded, all of it, with good looks and biceps to boot. There wasn't a single one of these men-women she couldn't arm wrestle down in a two-count.

The director paused. I can offer a few dollars. Not like before, however. Our budget's dwindling.

I'll take whatever your budget can allow me.

The director gave a single nod. Her attention drifted off. I have a cold, she sighed.

Self-pity won't help you now. You should have thought of that before you let her run her own little whorehouse.

What? I'm... oh...

Did you hear me? Jarmilla said.

What? The director blinked sleepily.

I've already got her, Jarmilla announced. She's sitting out in the lobby. Wait until I'm gone. And then you'd better grab her. She's a wild one, you well know, and might change her mind at any minute.

They can't live with us but they can't live without us, the director said. She seemed not surprised, not happy, not sad that their escapee had been returned, perhaps an effect of her medication. The few moments of silence dragged out with the thick slow motion of cough syrup. It's a symbiotic relationship, the director concluded.

If that's what you would like to think it's fine with me, Jarmilla said.

You two have always had a baffling connection, the director pondered.

It doesn't matter now, Jarmilla replied and stood up. I see you have a Negro guard. I hope you know what you're doing. On the way out of the building, she paused near Penny and leaned down. I'll be back in a few minutes, she told her. Stay here.

All right, Penny said.

1992
Lousiana

Now for the first time they were opening the gate and telling the live wire she could leave and the contrary fool wanted to stay. Jarmilla marched around the courtyard, intending to set the girl straight. She found her sitting in her own room with a companion. They were both in straight chairs, leaning forward. They were watching Oprah on the TV. Jarmilla pushed the open door wide. I see you're still here, she said.

The live wire turned toward Jarmilla and gave her an appraising shake of the head. She reached over and turned Oprah a little bit lower. It's free rent, she said.

You were always in such a fever to get out.

I can't now. She displayed her hands on each chair arm.

Jarmilla drew closer. It's just the left one. Looks like you had a slight brush with a buzz saw, that's all.

Him, she said, and Jarmilla saw that her companion's face was partly eaten away.

He's worse, Jarmilla agreed.

We're married.

Married! Jarmilla exclaimed. Since when? Why, you've got to be sixty if you're a day.

Fifty six.

Don't you think it's a little late for something like that?

We didn't want to have any children, the woman said. The man beside her chortled.

I'd say you're safe at fifty six. Well, fifty seven now, Jarmilla said. Happy birthday. You see I didn't forget you. Never do.

It's not my birthday, the woman said.

Jarmilla sat on the edge of the bed. It's not? she asked. But I always come on your birthday. All those parties I gave you. The picnic baskets I'd pack. We'd go swimming at the lake.

She stopped herself. She tried not to give away her embarrassment. She chewed on her lips and looked at the wall. TV Guide covers were taped up for artwork.

I guess you know your sister's dead, she said.

You told me that ten or twenty years ago. The woman turned back toward Oprah.

Jarmilla nodded, searching for other news. I like her, she said about Oprah, but they must not have heard. She hadn't even been introduced to the husband. Neither of them seemed very interested in her.

Penny had stayed at the leper farm ten months. They must have known she was an imposter but they let her stay until the live wire was returned. Then they forcibly ejected her, but still she didn't leave. She slept on the sidewalk and defecated on the grass. Leonard was home when they called to say what mental hospital he could find Penny in.

Jarmilla was sure this really hadn't happened, it was one of her dreams when she was feeling bad, but Leonard had taken the shovel and dug a hole wide and deep and into it he had thrown pots and pans and everything from their kitchen that had been a part of their traveling sales team, and then he had spit into the hole and then he had left.

The woman seemed much more interested in Oprah than in anything Jarmilla had to say. It didn't seem possible that this boring woman before her was the same febrile creature she had fought with all these years.

What's happened to you? Jarmilla asked.

The woman turned to look at her. She paused long enough for her eyes to narrow in appraisal, then went back to the TV. The same thing that's happened to you, the woman finally answered.

Nothing's happened to me, Jarmilla said.

The woman snorted, keeping her eyes on the TV.

Jarmilla waited until the show ended. Then she got up and turned off the TV. You have to leave, she announced. She cleared her throat and yelled out, You have to leave!

Both of them jerked. The man reached for the TV clicker but Jarmilla slapped it away.

She tried to explain it to them. Nurse Cora says they're just going to dump you on the sidewalk. Like they did your sister.

She never did understand why I wasn't glad to see her, the woman said.

She didn't understand much, Jarmilla said. She stood up. Well then, you'd better get packing. I told Nurse Cora you could come stay with me. He — she nodded toward the husband — he can stay shut up in the room if he doesn't want anyone to see his nose. There's work enough to be done inside.

Can I bring the TV? the man asked.

I've got one in my house, Jarmilla said irritably.

This would make two, the man said.

It's not yours to take! It belongs to them! Jarmilla felt the anger pounding in her head. She was too old now to suffer through another one of those headaches. Get ready! she screamed.

The woman got up and began untaping her TV Guide covers and carefully folding them into a stack.

Spring, 1963
Louisiana

For her birthday that year Jarmilla brought her another volume of the series. This one was *Great Irish Literature*. She'd already given *Great English Literature, Great French Literature,* and *Great German Literature* for other birthdays.

She found the girl sitting at the water fountain in the square, kicking up her legs. The white columns gave the illusion of a lazy plantation, and that's what the girl counted on. Jarmilla knew her tricks. The live wire just played along until it was time for another escape, splashing in the fountain, getting everyone lulled to sleep, and then presto, she was off and running.

For *me*, for my *birthday*? the girl mocked as Jarmilla held out the present.

Each year Jarmilla hoped the leprosy had rapidly progressed, providing her with some kind of validation. Each year the girl looked the same except insufferably prettier, and each year Jarmilla was confronted by the same fear, that she had condemned the wrong person to this place. What if someone had made the same mistake with Leonard?

When are you going to get me *Great American Literature*? the girl asked after ripping open her present.

I already have, Jarmilla huffed.

The girl started laughing.

Why are you laughing? Jarmilla demanded.

The girl muffled her mouth with both hands, which made the laughter sound snotty and coarse. She was shaking and kicking up her legs. No you haven't, she barely spit out, but I know why you think you have. I know why. I know exactly why. I need to tell you something: You're dumb, she announced with candid delight.

Jarmilla was completely bewildered, but she hid it with a threat. I suppose I'll stop coming after this, she told the girl.

Can you get me something else next year? Something about songs?

Songs? Jarmilla put as much derision as possible into a sniff.

Rock-n-roll stuff. With pictures.

You're too old for that. My god.

Well, then, a coloring book.

If you don't straighten up I'm leaving, Jarmilla warned.

The girl was wearing a loose smock and she looked much younger than twenty eight. Her legs were skinny and gnarly with muscle, like a ten-year old tomboy's. The knees had always been permanently discolored with a bruise-like darkness — also like a tomboy's — but this time they were dramatically scraped. The scrapes went all the way up her legs. New wounds, without time for scabs. They looked poisoned somehow, as if something suppurating and awful was getting ready to emerge.

My god, what did you do to yourself? Jarmilla asked.

I have a job, the girl announced proudly. She said nothing further. She was going to force Jarmilla to ask.

And doing what, might I inquire?

I'm training the police dogs. They set me loose in the woods and the dogs come find me.

That's insane. What would be the point?

They're practicing. Because someday it'll help a poor little girl who's really lost.

A poor little girl who's really lost. Oh for heaven sakes. You're either a saint or you're lying. I'm your only visitor, young lady, so straighten up and treat me with the respect I deserve.

It's true. Ask what's-her-name.

And what will what's-her-name tell me?

That it's true.

The policemen wouldn't let you do that, Jarmilla said.

Yes they would. They love me, the girl said. It's a real race to find me first. They like it late at night in the bushes. Under the trees. On the cool moss...

Don't talk like that.

It's true. They're not afraid, like you were. They say I'm hot as a stick of dynamite inside.

Good-bye, Jarmilla said, turning on her heels and striding away.

Is this forever? the girl called after her with a wild hoot.

Jarmilla was on her way to the director's office when, from behind, she recognized the heavy clipping on the Spanish tile. From the sound alone she could picture the director and the way she moved side to side in her forward gait. Just the clomping of her ineffectual stride made Jarmilla want to wheel around and let her have it. These administrators reminded her of Leonard's teachers over the years, plain absolute fools who should have been cobwebbed behind desks, doling out 1¢ stamps in a god-forsaken post office. Instead they were in charge of other people — and look what happened. There had already been two escapes and Jarmilla could sense a third one on its way.

I'm giving you fair warning about that girl, she blurted angrily to the director.

Oh Jarmilla, the director sighed. The war is over. She's happy now.

1992
Louisiana

Is this where you live? the man asked when she slowed down at the little white church and turned in. Jarmilla took a good look at his face in the rearview mirror. Termites couldn't have done a better job.

Is it eating his brain, too? she asked.

He just needs a schedule to stick to, the woman said.

I can give him that, Jarmilla said.

He'll still need certain shows to watch.

Did you ever know a little rich boy there?

What was his name?

I don't know, Jarmilla said. But he wore a velvet coat. Tucked his chin down into it.

Do you know anyone with a velvet coat? the woman asked her husband.

Jarmilla heard nothing from his side of the back seat.

He thinks it's a trick question, the woman said.

Jarmilla wondered what her son was doing today on his birthday. He was in a city somewhere living in a rented room. She hated thinking of Leonard on Sundays when the downtowns were empty and only the bums were out. Sometimes when she lay in bed, her bones aching, she was back in Oklahoma and she could hear him in the kitchen stealing sugar cubes. She would have never given him up no matter what disease he'd had. Not ever, not for anything. Didn't he understand that?

She didn't drive too far up the path. It was rutted and weeded. The little white church was scarred with graffiti. There was a big scorched circle in the yard and a blanket of beer cans.

Jarmilla got out and scraped her foot along the dirt but they had ruined everything and nothing was familiar. Maybe the boy told you about this spot, she announced. Right here somewhere, this was his spot, he was the first one. She spoke, but they weren't listening. Well, come on out and get the shovel, she ordered loudly. It's in the trunk, she told the man.

The man seemed to be handy with cars. He went right to the front seat and popped the trunk, but there was no shovel inside.

I always keep it in the trunk, she said. She marched over and had a look for herself.

Why do we need a shovel?

We need to leave it all behind, Jarmilla said. Throw all your diseased clothes down. Just throw them on the ground. All this blowing dust will cover them up by morning.

They opened their suitcases and scooped out yellow clothes and tossed them upwards into the air like rich people throwing their money. The woman started laughing and she laughed and laughed until she was forced to cover her mouth with both hands. The live wire in her returned and for a moment Jarmilla was reunited with that thirteen-year-old girl. The three of them got back in the car and now the man was behind the wheel with the woman in front. The Toyota lurched from side to side as he turned it around in the ruts. The man seemed to go sixty miles an hour down the gullied path. In the backseat Jarmilla could feel everything in double-time. She didn't look behind her as they turned out onto the road. She didn't want to see the churchyard on fire.